Sweet Lo

A billionaire cowboy with a huge crush on an intriguing store owner in need of his help…can West help Genna find more than she's asked for, with true love and a future with him?

Genna Barry grew up traveling the world with her parents but dreamed of settling down in a small town and making a life of her own. Now, as an adult dropped by the man she thought she loved, she's found Lone Star, Texas, and opened a real store to go with her booming online store. She's loving her life, a life that involves *no* dating because she's not willing to sacrifice the happiness she's found by being rejected ever again.

West Buckley admires the beautiful store owner and is highly infatuated with her, but word is she's not interested in dating anyone. So he's trying to hide how he feels and just be her friend—a hard task when his interest is so strong even his brothers see it.

When one of Genna's online clients wants to come to town and bring her single daughter to shop and hopefully meet some cowboys, West is pulled in to help. And hiding his feelings for Genna gets tougher.

Though he keeps the books for his family's huge ranch and likes raising cattle—he lives at his grandparents' old homestead and raises lots of goats, keeping his grandmother's favorite hobby alive—little does he know it's also a dream of Genna's...can it lead to the two of them finding love together?

Welcome to Lone Star, Texas: in this fun, inspirational romance series, you'll watch as each of the Buckleys find love in the small town, surrounded by wonderful people eager to see all of them happy. These are entertaining, emotion-filled love stories that will make you smile.

SWEET LOVE'N COWBOY

Billionaire Cowboys of Lone Star, Texas, Book One

HOPE MOORE

Sweet Love'n Cowboy

Copyright © 2022 Hope Moore

CHAPTER ONE

Genna Barry waited outside the dressing room of her store in Lone Star, Texas. It was the perfect spot for the online business she'd started several years ago. A year ago, she'd fallen in love with this place the moment she'd driven into town. Soon after, she'd opened the hardwood doors of Genna's Classy-Sassy Boutique, no longer just online but also solid and real, and a big thrill to her to walk inside of each day.

After having traveled the world with her parents pretty much her entire life, homeschooling until it was time for college, Genna dreamed of settling down and calling a small town home.

Her mother had told her stories as she grew up about a town in the middle of Texas, where she'd visited on vacation when she was a girl with her parents. The stories always stood out to Genna, of the cabin on a ranch they stayed in and the fun adventures her mom had there…especially with the baby goats that were raised on the ranch with the cattle and the fun entertainment they provided.

She'd built her online store while in college and gotten distracted by what she'd believed was love, and then she got engaged. They'd been engaged for three years while she ran her business online and adjusted her dreams for his, and then all of her happily-ever-after dreams crashed and burned when he found a new love and dropped her like a watermelon, cracking her heart and splattering her plans with the impact. She'd had it— her life was, as of that moment, up to her. So, the next day, she'd yanked her shoulders back, her chin up, and driven to the town she'd always dreamed about: Lone Star, Texas.

Trying to find love was off her map. She'd decided then and there that she was going to find a place to call home. Find a town that drew her and was full of people she enjoyed being around. She had a wonderful, successful online business, so that gave her the opportunity to choose, to pick the place that she would label home—a heavenly home on earth, so she'd driven here that day, parked her car on the main street, and took Lone Star in.

It was small but had a lot of shops, and many looked like secondhand stores full of all kinds of interesting things. Places she'd like to explore. They were exactly what she thought, and obviously people came from all over to spend a day or the weekend browsing through items. As she stood there, looking at the fronts of the stores, she knew without a doubt that this was her place. A smile bloomed across her face and heart...this was where she was supposed to be.

That first day she'd gotten out of her car, her thoughts racing as she studied everything, and in that moment two ladies walked out of the Mulberry Diner—two special ladies. They smiled and laughed as they started to cross the road, headed toward either Calhoun's Feed and Seed on the end of the street or Josie Jane's Wash and Repeat beside it. The bright-lemon paint made it very noticeable. But they saw her and suddenly stopped walking, turned and smiled at her.

The first lady had soft green eyes and a radiant smile. "Hi there. Are you looking for something in particular? We can help you. I'm Josie Jane Willis, and I own that store right there, Josie Jane's Wash and Repeat." She pointed to the bright-colored place across the street by the feedstore. "And this is Ruby Mulberry, and she and her husband Red own the diner." The diner was mulberry colored, obviously to match the name. "So, we're kind of used to being around here and know where everything is in and around our lovely little town."

Ruby's name also matched the last name—as did her husband's, Red—and all of it had Genna smiling.

As was Ruby, hugely. She flopped a hand to her well-rounded hip so hard her curling ponytail bounced. "And we like to welcome people to our town. If you want something to eat in a little while, we will be serving lunch soon. My husband is one of the best cooks in the world. And I mean it when I say that. It's not just because he's cute and I love him—he is a wonderful chef, and you can find out if you want to go in and test him out. Anyway, I don't mean to talk on and on.

Welcome to Lone Star."

Genna was smiling, inside and out. "I'm Genna Barry. I like y'alls attitude. I just came to town to check things out and I was, umm, thinking about finding a place to stay for a few days. Or maybe a month. I just need some time off, and my mom came here when she was young and always said it was a great little town. Her and her mom stayed at a cabin on a ranch and enjoyed it very much. So I decided I was due some vacation time to figure a few things out and here I am. I thought I'd see if this place was still as great as Mom remembered it being."

"Isn't that wonderful," Josie Jane cooed. "What was your mom's name? We might have known her since we've both been here our entire lives."

"They stayed at a little cabin on a place called Buckley Ranch. My grandma knew the owners. So they came and stayed, and Mom—Olivia—loved her stay while she was here and used to talk about what a fun place it was to enjoy being outside. She was from the city, so she liked roaming around."

Ruby tapped her cheek with her fingers, glanced at

Josie Jane, and then looked back at her. "I think the Buckleys used to rent some of their cabins out years ago to people they knew or were friends of friends."

"Still do, I think," Josie Jane added. "We're glad you came to our little town. So, you need a place to stay. Come over here to my shop where I have a place to sit down, and we can talk about this and help you out."

And she had followed them across the street and into that adorable resale shop, to the center where there was a circle of chairs set up, just like they were waiting for a group to gather and have a great conversation. And that was just what they'd done, Josie Jane had called the Buckley Ranch and before lunch Genna had a cabin to rent.

She'd moved into the cabin on the outskirts of the ranch. It was a short drive and down a dirt road. It was a cute, white house—not a wooden cabin like her mom had stayed in, but nice. It was quaint, with a living room, small kitchen, two bedrooms, a bathroom, and a small back porch with a beautiful view of gentle hills. She'd loved it. Absolutely loved it.

After a few days, she'd eaten a lot at Ruby's

restaurant and watched a bunch of cowboys coming in and out of that place. She met several of them but had no intentions whatsoever of starting to date again. She'd come here looking for a place to call home and had no intentions of messing that up with any problems with a man. No, this was her time to build her new life...her life. Then, as she'd walked out of the diner that particular day after visiting with Ruby and Josie Jane, she'd paused outside the empty building connected next door to the restaurant. It had old red brick and a large, wide window that looked like a display window. She leaned close and looked inside the building and saw the wooden walls, and an upper area at the back with stairs that led up to it overlooking the wide-open room. It snapped something inside her. As she stared in that window, a new dream sprang up inside her, and she made a decision right then and there to set her roots deep by opening a real red brick store in this town and really settle herself into the town.

And so, it had happened quickly, she'd found out who owned it and had it rented by the end of the next week to house her online business.

And here she stood inside her actual store. She'd hoped some of her online customers might want to take a trip to her physical store, and that had happened. But also, this town drew people to it, and they loved her store too. She loved being surrounded by the wonderful secondhand stores in town, and Ruby hadn't been fibbing when she'd told her on their first meeting that her husband could cook. Oh goodness, could he ever.

Red was amazing, so amazing that people drove to town just to eat his food. He helped Lone Star be the perfect place to eat and shop, so it had been right for her store.

As she stood there happy and smiling, the door to the dressing room opened and the customer she'd been waiting on came out beaming. Audrey was a petite lady and looked lovely in the soft blue pastel blouse and pair of white jeans she'd put on. The tone of the outfit highlighted her icy-blue eyes and soft gray hair, while the fit was perfect.

"Beautiful," Genna said, loving it. Audrey was in her late forties or early fifties and already bought several outfits, having first been an online client. And like many of Genna's online customers, she'd been excited to come to the *real* store. She'd driven all the way from the Dallas area, thrilled to learn the store was in this area because she had relatives who lived in a nearby town.

Now, she smoothed her shirt and smiled at Genna. "I love it. I'm going to buy it, and all the other wonderful things inside the dressing room I've tried on. But now we're going to take a picture, right? I'm now going to join the club of those who've made it to the physical store and get a picture with you."

Genna laughed in delight. "Yes, I always love getting a picture with my customers, and I'll post yours on my blog with all the others. It's so wonderful you want to and makes me happy I opened this actual store so I could meet you and my other online customers."

"We're all glad too. Being posted with you online is a treat, and I'm excited that I'm finally going to be one of the smiling customers on there." Audrey's smile was radiant with excitement.

Genna was still shocked by this reaction from her customers. "Are you going to get to go to some of the other stores?"

"Yes. My husband is already roaming through them. And also, my daughter is coming with me in about three weeks, so I'll be back and she can get a picture with you too. We'll stay with his sister over in Marble Falls unless I can find a bed-and-breakfast here in town to stay at, and then they could come stay here with us for our fun weekend."

She took a breath, then kept talking. "I really want my daughter to see your shop but also, I'd really like it if there was a event going on. You know, a street dance or a party, something to entertain her. She's single and is always looking for the wrong kind of man. I tell you, there are some wonderful-looking cowboys in this town. And so courteous. We ate breakfast over at the Mulberry Diner this morning and it was almost full of the handsome fellas, and that got me to thinking. I couldn't help but think one of them could maybe be my future son-in-law if I could get her over here."

Genna tried not to chuckle at the speed of words Audrey had spoken so quickly. "Well, we do have a dance here sometimes at the community center at the other end of town. I'll have to check and see when we may be having another one. You let me know when you're coming, and I'll let you know if me and the ladies in town can come up with something. I mean, if your daughter is able to attend. And if she happens to find someone who interests her, would it be a hard dating situation? I mean, does she live closer than you do?"

It was a serious question because yes, ladies could come and dance with the town cowboys—cowboys who always enjoyed coming to the dances considering the town was kind of out in the boonies and they worked long hours, especially in the summers, so going elsewhere to look for a mate was hard. Maybe they did need to have a few dances involving more than just townsfolk. She'd heard of other small towns in Texas that did this.

"She's actually looking to relocate. Maybe near our relatives in Marble Falls, that's not too far away."

Something in the sound of Audrey's voice made Genna feel pretty sure that she was worried. "Well, I hope it all works out for her." She said as they walked to the front window of the shop where the customers preferred to get their photo taken. There was a little of the incoming sunlight highlighting them and usually made a good picture. There were two mannequins in the window: one in a dressy outfit and one in casual, making a great background to entice more people to come see the shop if they were near enough.

She placed her phone in the long metal-armed holder, then she and Audrey locked arms and smiled for the camera. They laughed instantly after the snap.

"I loved that," Audrey said. Her expression said it was so true. "When will I see it online?"

"Tomorrow. I'll do it this evening if I don't get to it this afternoon, but I promise it will be up by tomorrow. And if I can say so myself, that outfit looks great on you, and it really will bring out the sparkling of your pretty eyes. Everyone will notice."

"I'm so happy. And I can already tell you that I have friends, not just my daughter, who will be heading this way. It's a wonderful trip. And I'm sure I'll find a bed-and-breakfast somewhere near. So, I'm going to give you my number and you can give me a call about the dance or whatever y'all can come up with and I'll set up our trip. I bet more people will come if you do that. Okay, got to go. We're going for lunch before we leave town. That place is delicious."

"I'll be in touch." Genna had been looking out the front window just as a large, shiny truck pulled into one of the parking spaces. Instantly, her gaze locked onto the driver, West Buckley. Her heart blasted into rapid beats and she quickly hurried to the counter before he spotted her gaping at him.

Behind the counter, she quickly finished ringing up the sale as Audrey changed back into the clothes she'd had on when she'd come into the store. After she came back out and handed her new clothes to Genna, she folded them and placed them in one of the bags as Audrey paid, and then she watched her customer leave.

Genna had pushed thoughts of West from her mind and now it twirled around ideas about a dance. It was a great idea; yes, they had them every once in a while but it was basically just for the people who lived in the surrounding area. But what if it was an invitation to those who loved to visit or were thinking about it? It would be a great opportunity for her and everyone in town to grow their business with visitors. As funny as it sounded, it would also be an opportunity for more people to get their picture with her—still hard to believe that was a strong selling point for her business, but it was true; they loved being on her website, and it delighted her.

It had actually been her first online customer to the store who wanted a picture with her and had given her the idea to post it on the site. Boom, her online customers had loved it. So maybe they'd like an opportunity to come to a dance. It was worth considering.

Being here satisfied her in so many ways—having a wonderful life, enjoying where she was in that life. But…sometimes being dropped by the man she'd thought she'd loved haunted her. Sometimes she found herself hoping for a *real* true love story of her own.

West Buckley instantly jumped into her thoughts again.

She did not want to go there. Yes, at a town dance a couple of months ago, she'd found herself watching West and wishing he'd ask her to dance. But he hadn't, and it was a good thing. She wasn't sure she could let her walls down and just needed to only think of him as a friend. West was a wonderful man, as good-looking as all of his brothers and cousins, so why was she drawn to him? If she let herself back out there, it could ruin her feeling of home sweet home. The store was doing so well and she was settled into her new life, and she didn't want anything to upset her comfort here in Lone Star.

No, she had a good life right now, and she wouldn't risk messing that up for anything. Dating was not on her agenda. But maybe helping others date was.

* * *

West Buckley sat at one of the front booths next to the window at the Mulberry Diner. He took a sip of his unsweet tea.

His older brother Ryder draped his arm on the back of the booth seat across from him and grinned. "So, do you see her yet?"

West glanced back out the window, down the sidewalk, even though he knew he shouldn't. He was sitting so he had a direct view of Genna's store entrance.

And just as he was about to yank his gaze away and look at his brother, Genna came out onto the sidewalk, turned, and locked her door. She had that look on her face that said she had had a good day so far. He knew it was true. Since he'd sat down, he'd seen a woman come out loaded with bags and grinning as she'd headed for the nice Suburban sitting in front of the store. She started piling the bags in the vehicle as a man came out of Josie Jane's Wash and Repeat secondhand store across the street and hurried to help her. They'd then entered the diner and sat over toward the back of the restaurant, talking up a storm. It appeared the woman had had a great time, and from the look on Genna's face, so had she.

He watched her now, expecting her to come to the diner also and maybe say hi, or maybe he could… *Or not.* Instead, she headed across the street, straight to Josie Jane's. He watched her cross, telling himself not to enjoy the way her hips swayed naturally in her white pants and her pretty, just below the shoulders brown hair with a sparkle of burgundy tone glistening as the sun shined down. The soft, silky material of the pale-green shirt she wore made her look like spring walking across that road. And without seeing her eyes, he knew they were a similar color of the blouse and were probably sparkling brighter than the blouse or her hair. The woman had a way about her that reminded him of a woman who had total self-confidence, loved the life she lived, and actually didn't need anything else. Everyone had noticed that she didn't date.

He'd already figured that out just watching her. They'd had a dance a few weeks ago, and he had to make himself not get out of hand by asking her to dance, making sure he didn't put himself out there and be one of the many she had rejected. He didn't want to risk it. He'd been there once...anyway, he wasn't ready for that again. And no matter how leery he was, obviously his brothers had noticed that the beautiful lady who owned the dress store had caught his attention. Not just a little but so much so that yes, when he entered the diner, he always requested the front booths at the window and always chose to sit on the side of the table that would give him the view of her store entrance so he could watch her enter or exit her store.

He yanked his gaze off where she'd disappeared inside the resale store and met his brother's knowing gaze. "Yeah, I think she's beautiful and to be admired. She's built a life she likes. I think that's cool. Awesome. We were born here. We like it here, but she chose it. Everybody likes her, and if you see people coming out of her shop, they are always grinning. You can tell that she likes to make people happy. So yeah, what about that?"

His brother leaned forward and put his elbows on the table, his clasped hands under his chin. "You need to ask her out, dude."

"I can't. I think she's made it quite clear that she's not interested in anybody. I'm not taking it as just me because she turned down everyone I saw ask her at that last dance we held at the town hall. She doesn't treat me any different than she treats anyone else. She's happy, and she's content, and it's very obvious that there's no opening in there for anything else. She's not interested in relationships."

His brother picked up his glass of water and took a sip, then set it down. "So that makes me wonder…seems kinda like it would make you wonder too…what happened to make her feel that way? She have something in her past that caused her to act like that? I mean, honestly, you know what that's like. And I do too. Anyway, I'm just telling you this because I'm like you. I'm not interested in anybody but it's clear in your eyes and your actions and with the way you talk about her that you are interested. It's time to step out there, brother."

He let his brother's words roll through his head just as—thank goodness—Ruby walked up to their table with their plates.

"Okeydokey, boys, I've got your today's specials all ready." She set the plates of hot roast beef, beautiful vegetables, and mashed potatoes with gravy before them.

"Your husband can cook. I'm telling ya, you married good." West laughed when she smiled at him.

"Honey, I know it. Because I get to bring these delicious meals out to everybody but I get to live with him and enjoy these meals every day. And I get to watch everybody smile when I bring their food to their table.

It just can't get any better than that. Well, every once in a while it can, when I help match somebody up." She dipped her chin and looked straight at him, and then glanced at his brother. And then she grinned wider and walked away.

"I don't know if you got the hint there," his brother said. "But I am not the only one who knows you sit on that side of this booth so you can watch her shop door open and close. You're watching to see when she comes out if she's coming in here or crossing that street to Josie Jane's."

Oh, brother. Was it that obvious that he liked the woman? He didn't say loved her; he just thought, like he'd said, he respected her. He thought she was awesome. What was wrong with that? Just tell him, *what was wrong with that?*

CHAPTER TWO

Genna opened the door and stepped into Josie Jane's store. If there was anyone who could help her figure out whether a dance for town visitors was a good idea, it would be Josie Jane. And of course Ruby, but she was really busy at the diner this time of day. She looked around the shop and it looked empty right now; lunchtime was a good time to talk. Then again, the shop had many aisles, so she could be wrong.

"Josie Jane, are you here?" she called.

"I'm near the rear. Come on back."

She followed the sound of Josie Jane's voice, toward the back, and in one of the nooks, found her setting an antique dining table with some pretty wine-colored dishes, as if getting ready for a meal. It was beautiful and enticing. One of Josie Jane's gifts.

"Hi there. I saw you were busy this morning," Josie Jane said. "Her husband was here and said his wife had been excited to come to your real store. Said she was a big shopper on your online store but had driven him crazy for a trip this way. They have kinfolks who live the town over but...he'd laughed and said that had just been an excuse to get her in your actual store."

Genna grinned. "I think he was right, and that thrills me. This town has just been a delight and blessing to me. Online stores are awesome, but meeting and greeting customers in person has a greater satisfaction for me."

"Me, too. I love my store. So, what brings you over?"

"I'm actually here because of them. His wife was wonderful and bought a lot of stuff. She's one of my online clients who couldn't wait to get here to get her picture taken and put on the website. Those pictures of me and my customers on my website was just an idea but it has really drawn women to my store. They get such reactions on my website, but she asked me an interesting question. She wants to know if, in a few weeks, we might be having a dance or a community gathering of some kind. She wants to bring her single daughter to town for a weekend to shop and have some fun. She's hoping to get her daughter interested in settling down. And if she can find a cowboy, Audrey thinks that would be wonderful." She chuckled. "Yes, it sounds funny. But wouldn't it be fun to hold a dance or an event that involves not just our town but our customers?"

"That's very interesting. It could be a draw to the town."

"Yes. I loved that last dance for the community, and knowing that it helped your granddaughter and Jace at the feedstore get back together after all these years was inspiring. So, what do you think—could we get something started like that?"

Josie Jane's green eyes were bright with interest. "You know, it sounds fun. And you're right, that dance helped those two to realize they were ready to get together. And if we hadn't had that dance when we did, they might not have realized that. So, yes, we need to do this. And we need to get Ruby involved. She will love this. I mean, seriously love it."

"I was thinking the same thing, but she's busy with the lunch crowd right now. Do you want to go have lunch?"

Josie Jane grinned. "I would love to. We can hint to Ruby that we have something great brewing when she takes us to our seats. And if there's time, she'll sit down and soak this up. Come on, let's go."

Genna followed Josie Jane to the counter, where she grabbed her key, and then led the way out onto the sidewalk. She turned her sign that said, Out to Lunch and locked up and then they headed across the street toward the diner. "Not that I needed to lock up. I'm not worried about someone stealing something, just me not being there if they need me."

Genna was chuckling at her words as they stepped up onto the sidewalk and her gaze locked with West Buckley's through the diner's windowpane. Her heart instantly thundered. *Stop it.* The words vibrated through her. She was not interested in him, even though just seeing him always caused her pulse rate to increase and her head to swim a bit. But it was lunchtime and she was with Josie Jane so she shoved the thoughts of West from her mind and focused on the open door that Josie Jane had pushed open and was holding for her to enter. She should have been the one to step to that door first and hold it for the older woman—not be rolling in unwanted thoughts about the good-looking cowboy. They entered the diner as her thoughts swirled.

"Welcome, you two. Come on in," Ruby called from where she'd been refilling tea glasses for a table of cowboys near the back. She hustled toward them, her bright-lime blouse shimmering over her full figure as it swayed over her black knit pants, and her sparkling sandals, with good arch support, tapped on the wooden floor as she approached.

It so pleased Genna that Ruby loved her clothing store and promoted it to people who asked her where she found her outfits. "You look wonderful today," she said when Ruby reached them.

"All because of you." She grinned, shot a hip out and propped her tea pitcher on it for a quick cute moment of fun. "I wish I could sit down and eat with y'all but it is busy today, Saturdays always are."

"Tell me about it," Josie Jane said as she leaned close to her friend. "We will have something to talk to you about when you have time."

Ruby instantly looked alerted. "Oh, really...now you've got my curiosity stirred up. I knew the minute I saw you two come in something was up, so yes, you fill me in the moment you can."

Genna smiled hugely. These two ladies were part of the reason she'd chosen to stay in this town and open a store for her online business. They were awesome and always made her smile. As they followed Ruby down the aisle by the front window tables, Ruby paused at West and his oldest brother Ryder's table. Looking at West, Genna's insides swirled.

"You fellas doing good?" Ruby asked, her gaze locked on West, who Genna realized had his gaze locked on her. "You need anything? I need to seat these two beautiful ladies, then I can come back and get y'all whatever you need."

Genna's heart went totally erratic as his emerald eyes held hers. "Hey, West," she forced the words out and yanked her gaze from his to look at his brother.

"And Ryder. Looks like you're having a great meal. Is that the special for the day?" No matter how much she didn't want to, her gaze flew back to West's wonderful eyes.

He nodded. "Yes," he said after a short hesitation. "And it's really good. We just got ours a few minutes ago and I'm already almost finished. You'd enjoy it if you ordered it. You, too, Josie Jane. Ruby's husband is an amazing chef."

"Yes, he is," Ryder agreed, drawing Genna's attention, only to find him studying her intently. "So, we saw you crossing toward Josie Jane's store earlier and you looked like you were on a mission. Now, here you are over here with Josie Jane in tow, who, as we all know, loves missions. So, is something going on?"

He was observant. Ryder was the oldest of the Buckley brothers, and now he was watching her.

"Well, I..." She looked at Josie Jane and then Ruby, who nodded, urging her on because she was curious too. "Let me just ask you guys this question. I had a customer earlier who was interested in having a dance or something like that that was not just for locals but for customers who are here for the weekend. My customers are also Ruby's and Josie Jane's customers. It would give them something to do in the evening. Do you think you guys or your friends would enjoy coming to a dance like that?"

West seemed to stiffen as she met his gaze. "The guys would probably like that. Cowboys work long hours, especially in the summer, so a gathering or dance would be good for them. You might have a successful dance or something fun. Don't you agree, Ryder?"

Ryder grinned. "Yep, I think that would be a winner because I know the last community dance was a hit. Y'all just figure it out and let us know. And if you want us to, we can ask around and see what kind of response we get. But I can already tell you it will be good."

Genna smiled. He was right, the idea *was* good. Then, whether she wanted it to or not, her gaze went right back to West. He was still watching her but she couldn't read his expression. She didn't want him reading hers either. "Thanks. Ruby better take us to our seats. I see more customers coming in."

Ruby grinned. "Okay, girlfriends. Follow me. And

thank you, fellas. You helped out a lot." And then she led the way to a table at the back of the diner.

They sat down in the comfortable chairs.

"Genna."

She looked over and saw her last client, and her husband was smiling too. "Hi, Audrey," she said.

"He loved my outfit," Audrey whispered loudly.

"I'm so glad, and I enjoy hearing that. And like I said, your picture will be on the website tomorrow."

"We will look. And also, that other thing we talked about...I'll be getting back to you on that."

Genna's lips curved up into another smile...seemed to be the only thing she could do lately. "We're going to talk about that and when you call, I'll have some information. Because if anything can be done, this gal here, Josie Jane, is the one who can do it."

Josie Jane chuckled. "Well, I hope I can. It sounds real interesting, and I think what you're wanting can happen. Thank you for suggesting this. I think it will be good for our little town."

Audrey beamed at that. "I am so excited. I hope it draws the interest of my daughter, who needs to have

her interest drawn somewhere. This is a lovely place."
She leaned closer. "And there are a lot of handsome
cowboys around here." She jerked her head in the
direction of Ryder and West.

And Genna was unable to not smile in agreement.

CHAPTER THREE

West tried not to look across the diner at Genna but found his gaze going there several times.

Ryder chuckled. "Give it up, man."

Feeling as if he'd been caught trying to steal a piece of candy, West glared at him. "Do you have a problem?"

His brother's lips hitched to a side grin. "No, you do. Come on, man, like I told you before, go ask the woman out."

West leaned to the side and pulled his billfold from his hip pocket. Then he pulled money for his meal out. Normally he would buy his brother's lunch too. Or vice versa. But today he was not buying Ryder's meal and not letting him buy his either, because he'd gotten too much fun out of drilling West where he knew West didn't want to be pushed. "It's time for work." He then got up and headed out the front door and straight to his truck.

He hopped into his truck as his brother followed him out the diner's door and paused to grin at him. West lifted a hand in goodbye and was glad they were in separate trucks with different jobs for the day. No way did he want to listen to Ryder's relentless words anymore today. His older brother had a way with bugging a guy to death if he got wind of something he thought was interesting. And it didn't matter whether it was true or not; he enjoyed pushing the limits. Without another glance at the diner or the store, he backed out, wanting to leave before Genna happened to walk out from inside the diner.

He was repairing a fence today on the far side of the ranch, where they had been notified by their neighbor that there was a hole they might want to look at and fix. Thankfully, there were no cattle on those acres at the moment, so that was one problem that was alleviated. He enjoyed fixing fences. His main job was keeping the books for the ranch, keeping track of profit and loss and everything in-between. Like him, all his brothers and cousins had something they really enjoyed and something they didn't. West was quieter than the others and didn't mind being alone in the office or fixing a fence by himself. Not that he was a complete loner; he just didn't mind when he was alone. So, he'd immediately volunteered to take care of this because it fit him so well and he had been ready to be out of the house on a Saturday afternoon.

Ryder was the opposite: disturbingly outgoing sometimes and enjoyed things that had a lot of people involved in them, especially if it had to do with a horse. But he was great at helping a horse that needed breaking or needed riding or healing…that was what his brother loved. And it was a good thing to love because when you had a bunch of horses as they did, something was always going wrong with one of them. And then there were the cattle. All of his other brothers were into fixing the cattle up.

Whereas West…well, he enjoyed everything, but fences could be repaired alone and that was one of the things he liked the most.

He watched as the end of town came up, and he

goosed the gas pedal and picked up speed. It was eleven miles to the dirt road that led to the piece of the ranch with the downed barb-wired fence. He hadn't even told Ryder what he was doing today because he knew after what had just happened in the diner, he'd have been really put through hot water. If his brother realized he was going out today to repair a fence near Genna's cabin, which she rented from the ranch, his brother would have not let up. It wouldn't have even mattered to Ryder that West was going while Genna was at work so she wouldn't even know he'd been out there. Ryder would have given him a hard time anyway and gotten some big laughs from it.

Didn't matter—West would have fixed the fence near her place or all the way on the far side of the big ranch. Their ranch was huge, and it dipped and spread out so that driving from one end to the other was a long drive. But nope, this fence problem was at the far edge of the pasture, where Genna's cabin sat and that would have been all Ryder would have concentrated on.

It was one o'clock as he reached the dirt road, he glanced at his watch again; about ten minutes had passed. He would be long gone before Genna closed her doors this afternoon at five o'clock and headed home. He drove a long way down the dirt road, similar to the road his old homestead house was on but on different sides of the main ranch area. He passed the cute cabin she rented and a flicker of wistful longing for her to be there hit him. He yanked his gaze forward and did not look back at the welcoming sitting area she'd set up at the edge of the house. A very obvious place to watch either sunrises or sunsets from one spot.

She'd recently asked Ryder whether it were for sale and been told it wasn't. But when Ryder had told him she'd asked, it had sent a blast of happiness through West because it meant she was staying in Lone Star, and he liked that. Liked it a lot.

He knew she was in town almost every day of the week and she closed her shop around four on Saturdays, from what he'd observed when he was in town across the street at the feed store or at the diner getting something to eat. But she always took Sundays off and sometimes Mondays. At least, that was what he'd noted as he'd watched her. Knowing all this was one reason he'd chosen to come today and fix the fence, she would still be at work.

His gaze went back to the cabin. It was a nice place and she'd put some colorful metal chairs that he suspected she'd bought at Josie Jane's store. The older lady had probably painted the chairs herself. There was also a metal table sitting in front of them and a couple of very colorful flowerpots beside them. The things she'd added to the house had made it much more inviting than before she'd moved in. They'd just let people stay there for the weekends so hadn't worried about giving it a homey or inviting look like it was now. He wondered what it looked like inside or out in the back yard where they'd put a wooden picnic table— she'd spruced it up like she had the front yard. Just looking at it now drew him to wanting to sit down and relax.

Get hold of yourself, West.

He shook his head and gassed the truck and drove on by. Just twenty feet past the house, he pressed on the brake and slowed down as he whipped the truck onto the dirt road entrance, where the metal gate blocked his approach. Shoving the gear into park he hopped from the truck and unlocked the fence, pushed it back, and then hurried back to his truck and pulled in past the gate. Knowing there were no cattle in the pasture, he left the gate open and drove across the pasture toward the fence. He saw it before he got too close. It was down, all right. The people who owned the property on the other side of the fence were the grandchildren of the rancher who had run it all his life until he'd passed away a few years ago. The family still came out to the ranch sometimes; even though they didn't raise cattle, they enjoyed the place. They knew if they ever wanted to sell it that all they had to do was offer it to them and they'd buy it.

As he looked, it was clear that the fence had been damaged. An oak tree on this side of the fence had fallen and destroyed the section of fence. He had more work than anticipated but thankfully he had all the gear he needed in the bed of the truck.

He climbed out of the truck, taking his gloves with him, and strode to the tree and fence. He had his work cut out for him. The tree was thick and had a lot of limbs. It was going to get done; it was just going to take longer than he'd expected.

He walked back to his truck, pulled his tailgate down, and reached for his saw. Thankfully it wasn't a gigantic tree but at least fifteen feet tall, with wide limbs that spread between his ranch and theirs. He was glad they happened to be here and riding on their four-wheelers and saw it. Cows had already been scheduled to be moved to this pasture tomorrow and that would have meant having to hunt them down on the other property.

He got busy.

Three hours after he started he was sweating from the heat, he lifted a bottle of water and took a long drink. He stared at the limbs he'd cut and piled to the side, and then his attention was drawn by the sound of a car. He turned and saw Genna turning in to the drive of her cabin. He shot a glance at his watch, realizing she'd closed up a little early.

His gaze followed her as she drove up the drive. Suddenly she stopped, as if spotting someone in the pasture. He lifted his hand, knowing she would recognize the ranch's truck, considering it had their name and brand on the side. Hopefully she'd see that it was him despite the distance between them and not worry that someone who shouldn't be here was in the pasture. She climbed out of the car, then walked over to the fence.

"*West,* is that you?" she called, placing her fingers around the top row of wire on the fence.

She'd recognized him even at this distance. Just the idea of it pleased him. He and all his brothers had a resemblance, but she'd known it was him standing here. "Yes, I'm cutting up a tree that fell."

"Okay...do you need help?"

He chuckled. "No, I don't think I need you. I can handle it."

She shifted and popped a fist to her hip. She looked cute but her stance made him think she was aggravated by his answer. "So, you don't think I can help you?"

Her challenging words had him suddenly feeling bad about laughing. "Sure, come on over and help if you want to."

A beaming smile flowed across her face, and his stomach dropped to his boot tips with a bang. From this distance, that smile had done that to him and in the diner, it caused his insides to shift like sugar sifting through fingers. But here, out in the boonies, with just the two of them, just knowing he'd caused that amazing smile made it strike all the deeper. He swallowed hard because his mouth had just gone desert dry. He just stood there mesmerized.

"Great," she exclaimed. "I'll be right there. I have to change but I'll be quick."

He watched her spin and trot back around to her driver's side, slip behind the wheel, and move her car to the edge of the house. Within moments, she was inside, the breeze having caused her pretty hair to wave at him as she rushed up the three steps and into the house. He could not imagine the beautiful clothing store owner even wanting to come out here and help him clean up a tree. It was mind-boggling.

Maybe she would just carry branches…heck, he didn't care; just having her out here beside him was something he hadn't imagined would happen. It was like a dream. And who knew whether she would be good at cleaning up a tree or not—she could totally surprise him and be great—not that he cared one way or the other.

What he cared about was that he was about to get to spend some time out here alone with Genna.

His throat grew dry again as he heard a door slam and he looked back toward the house. She'd already made it to the fence—obviously having jogged to get there that quick. He watched as she bent over at the waist and stuffed her first leg through the two middle rows of wire and then carefully maneuvered her torso through the two wires, then straightened up as she pulled her other leg through to join the rest of her body. Smooth and easy and no climbing the fence involved. Now, she didn't waste time but instantly jogged across the pasture, her brown hair glinting reddish in the sunlight.

Beautiful…just beautiful.

His gaze had frozen on her. She'd changed into jeans and boots and a soft green T-shirt, and he was a frozen man as he watched her come toward him.

Get your head on straight, man!

"Okay, show me where you need me." She came to a halt right in front of him. She swept the loose hair from her forehead as it had swung forward at her abrupt halt.

He grinned. *Man, this woman was something…everything about her was—* "Sure," he said, cutting off his thoughts. "Do you want to cut some limbs with the saw or pick up the ones I've cut? What would you like to do?" There, at least he sounded normal. Well, fairly normal—hopefully she didn't notice the faint uncontrolled waver of the last word which went slightly higher then slid downhill. Thankfully at the end of the sentence so it ended quickly.

Her eyes grew brighter than normal as she looked from him to the tree, making him unsure if she'd heard his voice waver. She laughed, staring at him as her eyebrows crinkled. "What would I like to do?" she repeated his question. "Well, I don't know. I'll do whatever you want me to do. Do you want me to pick up the wood? I used to help my stepdad pick up wood when he did the yard, when we were actually home and not traveling. When we traveled, someone else did the yard. Truth is, we weren't home that much."

He found her words intriguing and they relieved him because she didn't sound like she'd noticed his odd voice seconds ago. Also, he knew from the little gossip that went around that she'd chosen this town because her mother had once stayed here on the ranch in one of these cabins when she was young. And that fact had been what had brought Genna to town and she'd quickly settled into the cabin and opened her store.

"How about you just help me by stacking the wood I cut. When you get tired, you're free to stop. Tomorrow, after church I'll bring my trailer over here and load it up. This wood will work as firewood for the main house and cabins. I'll put some over there at your cabin since you may want a warm fire this winter."

"Oh yes, thanks so much. That would be nice to have a fire in the fireplace this winter. I'll go get busy now." She started to walk toward the wood but paused. "You look kind of tired. Are you going to stop soon?" Her gaze dropped to his T-shirt. "You've sweated a bit so obviously you've been out here a long time." Her gaze came back to his, and his heart pounded like it was cracking firecrackers.

"Yep, been here since I left the diner."

"Oh, wow, outside in this heat that makes a long

day. No wonder you look…hot, and a bit tired. Don't you think you can just come back tomorrow and finish it?"

Having seen her gaze stall on his clinging T-shirt had him suddenly wanting to pump his fist in the air and let out a yelp of triumph. Could she be interested in him? He was in shape and yes, sweating made his shirt show off his muscled chest. He yanked his thoughts back to her question. "No, I need to get it fixed so cows can come out here soon. It was supposed to be tomorrow or Monday but looks like Tuesday will be the day."

"I see." She picked up one and then another piece of wood, holding them on her hips as she walked over to where he'd been piling them. She let one drop from her hips onto the pile, then grabbed the other with both hands and neatly set it on the ground and straightened up the one she'd dropped.

She turned back around and caught him still staring. *Goodness, the woman was beautiful.* But he wasn't going there. "I-I'm about to start this thing, so don't let it scare you."

Her stunning smile bloomed. "Thanks for the

warning. I'll stay out of your way."

And she did just that. He forced himself to turn away and start cutting, thankful at least that with the saw going, he didn't have to have a conversation with her, nor could he stare at her any longer. But after a while, he'd cut the large tree trunk into segments and then cut several of the segments into log-sized pieces and it was time to take a break and get a drink. He turned off the saw and turned around.

"Whoa," he said, stunned by her work. She had carried almost all the previously cut lumber to the piles he'd started. And she'd stacked it all neatly and was still going, arms now unloaded. As she turned and found him watching her, he saw that she didn't look worn out in the least.

He strode toward the truck, removed his hat from his head and lifted his forearm to use the sleeve of his shirt to wipe his damp brow. Then he replaced the hat and opened the ice chest. "Are you ready for some ice water?"

She grinned. "I'd *love* one. I was wondering how

you could keep going with that heavy saw and not take a break."

The woman had a wonderful grin. A beautiful smile and enticing eyes, he thought as he pulled a bottle out of the ice and held it out to her. Their fingers touched as she reached for it. Fire, hot fire, shot through him, as if he'd been blasted by the sparks from a furnace.

She paused, her eyes flaring too. "Thank you," she said, stepping back as she quickly twisted the lid off her bottle.

He grabbed himself a bottle and pretty much tore the lid off before tilting the drink up as he started gulping the water. He held it straight up and let it flow into him, hoping it would calm the fire he suddenly had burning through him.

What had just happened?

CHAPTER FOUR

Genna took two gulps of the chilling water, grateful to have it in her hand after the heat that had shot through her when her and West's fingers had touched. Never had she felt an electric sensation or fire like that just from touching someone's fingers—or anything else, for that matter.

Her thoughts swam, realizing his touch had shocked her more than any kiss she'd ever gotten from *anyone*. Even the man she'd been engaged to just over a year ago.

Her gaze locked with his, and he looked alarmed. *Had he felt it too?*

If so, it was completely obvious he did not like it. *Wow, this was odd.*

Alarm rang through her; she couldn't just throw the

bottle down and stomp toward her cabin—or run to it. After all, he was a nice guy; she just wasn't ready to feel anything from a man again, nor upset one as he looked stung or something. Besides what did that matter? She didn't need a man or want one. She was happy. She loved her business. She loved where she was living. The people she shared a town with. No, she wasn't interested in changing things up. So why had his momentary look of shock or displeasure bothered her? Or was it her imagination?

She glanced at him again. He'd finished one bottle of water and reached for another. He had been working and the sweat dampening his shirt showed it even more now. He'd been excellent as he'd held that saw and sliced through the thick tree trunk like he was cutting up cheese wedges. Other than the sweat, he hadn't looked like it was work as she'd seen his muscular arms show their power—though she'd only glanced at him a few times, trying not to stare, she'd noticed it all. *Still* felt his touch of moments ago.

Her staring of itself should have been a warning that she was drawn to him more than she'd realized.

Yes, she'd thought he was good-looking and when she looked at him now her insides were feeling like nothing she'd ever felt before. This reaction she'd just had—was having still...*what in the world?*

She needed to find something to say. Her brain tried to work but it was stuck, just locked on the feel of his hand on her and the thundering of her heart and her bombarding of feelings stomping over her.

"Did y'all..." he started, his voice drawing her gaze.

She saw that he'd paused drinking his water to ask her the question. She waited.

"Did y'all come up with a plan for the dance y'all were talking about?" He swallowed once more, then set his bottle on the tailgate of the truck. Then he yanked his hat off, rammed his hand through his wavy dark hair, and set it back on his head at an angle.

An angle that shadowed his eyes, making it so that she couldn't see the glistening emerald of his eyes. But at least he'd given her something to talk about, so she forced words to come out, and to sound normal. "Yes, we set a date, and we're going to have a community and customer weekend. Josie Jane was thrilled about the idea, so then we asked Ruby and Red how they felt about it and they loved it too. So, we're doing it in three weeks." Thank goodness her excitement of the event helped her get hold of herself. "It will take us that long to get ready for the dance. They are telling all the businesses in town so they can send an email to all their customers, me included, and then we can know about how many to expect in the next week and we can start planning. I think it could be good."

His brows had dipped as he stared at her. "Do you think there will be a lot of people responding?"

"I hope so. We were thinking about closing off the main street and having a street dance. It's larger and people can see all the stores, and if store owners want to leave their store open, they can do business or they can just attend the dance. It's an option but could be a good one."

He crossed his arms. "That would be a lot of people in town, maybe it will just be a nice group of people and not a bombarding."

"Are you afraid of a bombarding?" Her gaze bore

into him, trying to read him. "You do seem like a quiet man, but I don't think you're shy. Just processing?"

A grin spread instantly across his handsome face. "I'm not shy. I speak up when I need to or want to. I'm not afraid of people and I speak up if needed, so I don't classify as shy. Just not always the best talker who doesn't mind spending time alone."

"That's exactly like I thought. So what about the gathering?"

"I enjoy when the town has their community gatherings, I'm just not sure about one with lots and lots of strangers."

She liked the way he talked. She pushed the thoughts of what was worrying her and the reaction of her skin from his touch aside. She was not a weak person. She had survived a wimpish fella who she'd thought loved her, and she had decided that would never happen again. But that didn't mean she was just going to close the door on every aspect of attraction. Because yes, she could not deny that she was attracted to this handsome, *nice* guy—cowboy. This long, tall Texan who lived in Lone Star, Texas. She smiled.

"What's got that big smile on your face?" His lips curved up at the edges.

Shoot. "I…was just kind of hearing a song in my head as I was looking at you."

"You were thinking of a *song* while you were looking at me?"

She laughed, loving this instead of being leery. "Yep, my own tune. I looked at you, and I thought about a long, tall Texan who lives in Lone Star, Texas. Want me to sing it to you?"

His smile widened across his face and he chuckled. "Okay, so you have a big imagination, obviously."

"Only when I'm inspired. It's like my clothes in my store. When I see them, I know…" *What was she saying?* That when she sees the clothes, she knows? So, when she sees *him* she knows. *Knows what?*

His brows met. "Um, I don't see myself looking like a dress or a pants suit."

She busted out laughing. As much as she'd said a very odd thing just now, this was hilarious. "No, you're right. Sometimes I just say really silly things. And I don't actually plan on it but things just roll out of my mouth, like that description. It's something I'm known for that I don't truly want anyone to know about, so I fight it off. And today I didn't win." She really didn't do it much but right now it was a way to downplay what she'd said without meaning to.

He laughed, a low rumble that sent her pulse up a few notches. "Well, I hate to tell you, but I now know it. Know it all."

She stuffed her hand on her hip like she'd done when she'd first seen him across the fence. "And I hope you'll keep that to yourself. People will slowly but surely—if I talk to them enough—realize that every once in a while, something stupid comes out of my mouth. But you don't have to be the one to spread that bit of gossip."

He laughed again and her pulse kept climbing.

Goodness, the man was so good-looking when he laughed. His smile spread across his face, his eyes danced—the color was awesome emerald, sparkling in the sunlight because he leaned his head back and the sun caught them. *And here she was, staring at him with...* She slammed down her thought. "I better get back to stacking this wood if I'm going to get through. I have some paperwork to do and a photo to load to my website. My customer is anxious to see her visit to my shop on my site."

"You can go any time you need to. Really. You've helped me more than I anticipated and entertained me too." He chuckled again. "And I am not lying about any of that. You carried a lot of wood today and still have a great sense of humor. Are you tired?"

She lifted her arm up and flexed her muscle. "No, I'm not tired. I'm a strong girl. I work really hard at it." She grinned at him. It was true; she lifted weights every other day. Not because she wanted to build a massive body but because she liked having strength. One never knew when they needed to be strong…and not just in muscle but in attitude and decision-making. That had been the thing that drove her and enabled her to decide what her own life was going to be instead of just following her mom and stepdad around the country. She loved them both, but she'd just needed to settle down, make a home while they loved to travel.

She smiled at him. "I'll carry this little bit I have

here over there and add it to the stack, then I'll head toward home. It's going to be a gorgeous sunset tonight."

He looked toward the lowering sun and nodded. "Looks like it." He started toward the chainsaw, but turned back toward her. "When you get ready to stop, I will, too, and I'll drive you over to the cabin. No need for you to walk across that pasture again. Then I'll come back tomorrow and finish. Really, thank you. I enjoyed having company while I did this."

"You're welcome. I enjoyed it too." And she had…maybe too much.

* * *

West pulled the truck to a stop a few minutes after they'd decided to quit for the day. He stared at the cabin Genna lived in, still enthralled by her decorations. "You made this place look great. That's a very welcoming sitting area you've created." He met her gaze, and his heart did a hard thump as she looked away from him and at the sitting area.

"I love it. I sit out there a lot in the evenings when I get home. I bring my coffee or my tea and some homemade cookies or pie out there and I relax and enjoy it." She looked at him. "Would you like something to drink? Maybe sit out there for a few minutes and experience that enjoyment and the beauty of your land? That sun lowering behind those soft clouds is going to produce a beauty in a short while."

His pulse increased and he tried to focus as his index finger tapped on the steering wheel. Watching a sunset with her was almost irresistible especially since he really wanted to sit out there, but should he?

"Oh, you don't have to," she said, her voice odd. "I was just offering...but I do have some fresh tea in the refrigerator. Or I can make some coffee, won't take but a few minutes. And I have homemade chocolate chip cookies from last night's cooking spree. I have to say that I'm pretty good at making chocolate chip cookies because the recipe from my grandma is wonderful. I'm sure your grandmothers had wonderful recipes too."

Goodness, she was something. An unstoppable smile burst across his face. "Well, with that kind of invitation, I'd be stupid to say no. So yes, since I haven't sat down since lunch this all sounds too tempting to say no."

Her eyes faltered but she smiled. "Then come on. You can come in while I get it ready or go ahead and sit out here. Whichever one you want, I won't be long. That sun will be setting and it's a great view from those chairs that I've angled just right for watching the sun go down or the sun come up, depending which way you look or what time you sit down. If you're hungry for something more than chocolate chip cookies, I made some fresh tuna fish salad yesterday, and I could fix you a sandwich."

She stepped out and closed the door, and he did the same. They walked to the front of the truck.

"Honestly, a tuna sandwich is one of my favorites, but I'll just have a couple of cookies and a cup of coffee, if that's okay."

"You sound like me. I love a coffee in the evening, and cookies can't be beat. I'll be right back...unless you're hot and want to come in?"

"Nooo." He hemmed and hawed on wanting to go

in and knowing he didn't need to. "I'll sit out here."

She went in the house, and he sat down in the red metal chair and waited. *What was he doing?* He should have gone on home but no, here he was. He hadn't...well, he wasn't going there. He had been halfway able to talk to her today after they'd worked together for a bit. He hadn't thought it would be that way. But today he'd been more drawn to her than ever. *And was he going to try to go with it and see what happened?*

Or was he going to be a big chicken?

It had been a very long time since he had actually been drawn to someone like this...a very long time. The sound of a hoot owl hooting in the distant trees drew his attention and he let out an exasperated sigh. He knew that one day, if he didn't step out and try an actual relationship again, he'd be that stinking owl stuck out in the woods all alone.

"Okay, here I come," she called, her voice carrying on the slight breeze like a soft bird singing, drawing his gaze from the nice view to her ever enchanting face.

He was in trouble, and he knew it.

She, somehow or another, had exited the house carrying a metal tray with a couple of big mugs and a plate of cookies. There was also sugar and cream containers. He spurred himself with imaginary spurs and jumped up. "Here. Let me help you."

"I've got it. I am capable of carrying a tray. Now, sit back down and relax."

He grinned as he sat. "I honestly didn't mean to make it sound like you couldn't carry that tray. I was just trying to help you."

She chuckled as she set the tray on the small table. "I know. And I'm trying to help *you* relax." She hitched a brow at him.

This time he chuckled. "Got it." Grinning, he looked at the cups. "Wow, those are some really entertaining cups you have there, and some tempting cookies."

She settled into the yellow metal chair that sat next to his red chair, they were both slightly angled so that they had a look at the same scenery and each other for conversation and across from them were a pink chair and a blue chair, all very colorful. She reached for a bright-pink napkin on the tray and handed it to him. Then pointed at the four-inch-tall mug that was bright pink with a large handle, making it easy to hold.

The grinning white goat on the cup, with huge blue eyes, stared at him and he stared back, startled at her choice of cups. "I have to say, he's not the only goat to look at me that way."

"Cute isn't it?" She laughed as she picked up her cup and looked at it then at him. "I have this fascination with coffee mugs of all sorts. When I saw these two sitting on a shelf, I bought them instantly because I simply *love* goats and all their cute antics."

His infatuation skyrocketed at her words. "Really?"

"If you'd come into my kitchen, you'd have seen I have an outrageous habit of collecting funny, cute cups. And these goats are some of my favorites. I really, *really* adore goats, baby goats especially."

Excitement filled him as he grinned at her. "So, you like goats—*really* like goats?" He hitched a brow.

She cocked her head slightly to the side. "Yes, I do. They are adorable as babies and then just delightful and sweet as they grow. Watching them climb up or onto whatever is available and romp around with each other is just so fun. Watching them run and jump and nudge each other tickles me. Their energy is unbelievable and everything about them makes me smile."

He smiled, knowing she was about to be really surprised. "That's great—" he started but she kept talking.

"As a matter of fact, when I eventually buy my own place—I'd buy this place if y'all wanted to sell it to me with a couple of acres or so—anyway, I'm going to get some goats of my own. I love food and lotion and other things made with goat's milk so would enjoy not just their fun adventures but that too. There are just so many things about goats that I love." She sighed as she lifted her coffee.

He reached for a chocolate chip cookie. "Do you know I *raise* goats out on our ranch?"

She gasped. "*No*, I didn't know. Really, I thought it was a cattle ranch?"

"True, we have cows and horses and they're our top dollar makers, but we also have a lot of goats, a few pigs, chickens and some donkeys. We like fresh items, too, but I have to say we have never made things with goat's milk. They're just really good at eating grass on fence lines and things like that. But I have to agree with you, I like watching them run around and mess with each other. Climbing on top of things, I think, is their favorite thing. I made a sort of playground when I was younger that they still love. And of course, we do sell them, like you said, people like to buy goats. They're not our big moneymaker but they run in our family. My Gram loved them, and so does my mom."

"Really, how wonderful. And it's wonderful that you're keeping their love alive."

"Exactly my goal." He smiled at her, the fact that she'd known what he was doing touched him deeply. "I tell you what—when you want some, you just let me know and you can pick out however many you want. Though you're not home all that much, but we could fence you off a little spot for them since there's nothing here that would keep them in. I have to say, about selling one of these cabins…it's not something we've ever thought about. They've been here so long. But I can mention it to the guys. It is on the edge of the property—

you've got me thinking. But wouldn't you rather have a home? That's a really small cabin."

"Well, you're actually right about that. But I do enjoy living out here right now. And as much as I would love to have some cute goats out here with me, you're right, I'm not home enough to take care of them." She smiled. "But, I would love to come see yours. I'm excited."

He was, too, to be frank. "You just tell me when and you can come out anytime. When you're closed or in the evening after closing. I can come pick you up and take you out there or meet you there."

He took a bite of his cookie and was blown away by how delicious it was. The chocolate melted in his mouth and blended with the other flavors. *Amazing.*

"You like it, don't you? It's my gram's recipe. My mom only knew her mom a little while before she died, but she knew how to make chocolate chip cookies and she taught my mom, and she taught me. Even when we were doing all that traveling all over the place, she would bake those chocolate chip cookies and we loved to eat them together. I bake all kinds of cookies now but those are my favorite."

He leaned back in his chair with his coffee and cookie, really enjoying himself. This was the first time they'd ever sat together and had a talk like this. "I'm glad she taught you because I'm thoroughly enjoying them. My mother is a good baker too and enjoys cooking. She did a great job but since she's been traveling with my dad, we haven't been getting her cookies like we used to, so this is really nice."

"So, they travel like my parents. Well, my mom and stepdad, they love to travel and don't really have a place they call home." She had leaned back too, took a sip of her coffee.

"Really, well mine love it too. What about your real dad—what does he do?"

She traced a finger around the top of her mug and looked out at the setting sun. "I never met him. He died before I was born but Mom told me about him—" She looked at him then. "John was his name and I claim him even though I never met him. He's always sounded like a nice guy and mom always said if he were alive they'd still be married...but then, she wouldn't have had Brian and she does love him deeply. Life is complicated and as far as I can tell we are blessed to take it the way its handed to us. Find our happy ending and not take what we've had for granted. That's my mom, she took what life gave her, loved my dad and Brian and with good reason, he's wonderful to her and for her. I love him and am grateful she has him. He was good for me too, so, if I couldn't have my daddy I'm glad I've had Brian or dad as I call him. But anyway, tell me about those goats out there on your ranch. I think I'm about to start calling it a farm instead of a ranch since you have such a variety of animals out there."

He knew a distraction when he heard it but let it go, he wished she'd known her dad but was glad her stepdad had loved her and was a good man. "Actually, it was my grandmother, my Gram who started all that. My granddad, or Gramp, was a rancher, and my Gram came from a farm. Her daddy raised all kinds of animals and crops. They sold veggies, fruit, milk, and eggs, and even desserts and breads. That's how they made their living, so it was a combination when those two fell in love and married they kept both their legacies alive."

"That is so wonderful," she said, her voice soft as if in awe.

"Yeah, and we keep it up—not that those crops are our big thing, or goats, but we keep them going to carry on their legacy. And we all enjoy it. Like you say, it's one thing to watch a horse run and frolic but it's another to watch a goat running and romping around and kid around so much the name fits great. They're hilarious."

She laughed. "I know. I adore watching them online. I tend to pull up videos people post of them and it's just entertaining."

"I don't watch them on video but from my porch or in the yard with them. And one day—if I have kids, if I ever get married—I guess if that happens to me, I'll have kids who will enjoy it as much as I did."

"*Swweeeet,*" she cooed, her eyes sparkling—his stomach cartwheeled.

She was sweet, that was for certain.

Her expression instantly changed from a smile to a muted expression. She looked away from him and down the road. "I mean, sweet for you when you get married and have kids. They'll love it. Me, I don't know if I'll ever even think about getting married again. It's a rough ride when you have the rug pulled out from under you on the wedding issue. I didn't enjoy it, wasn't in control, and don't believe I'll ever chance it again. But I'm always happy for those it works out for. But I like control of my own life."

She was being very open about herself right now. And he was *very* interested in what she said—unlike what he'd thought, she wasn't just a great businesswoman concentrating on building her business. No, she'd been dropped by the man she loved and she'd slammed the doors of her heart closed after that.

And it sounded as if she'd placed a thick, strong lock on her heart.

CHAPTER FIVE

She'd said too much. Genna's heart pounded as she'd realized how she'd opened up as they sat here. "I love what I'm doing. It's not like I'm looking back with regret. And when you asked me to come see your cute little goats, well, my answer is yes. I would love to see them." His lips turned up into a smile and she was glad she'd changed the subject from the direction the other conversation was going to.

"Well, are you going to church tomorrow? If you are, then maybe after church I can come pick you up. You are closed on Sundays, right?"

"Yes, I am. I know it's a busy time for weekend

shoppers, but I enjoy going to church when I can and taking the afternoon off. So…" She paused. *Was she really going to do this?* "I would enjoy seeing the goats."

"Great." He stood. "I'll head out now so you can get that post on your website set up and then how about say…two o'clock—one-thirty, whatever works for you. Church is out about noon, or I could take you to lunch after church."

Lunch with West sounded more wonderful than she wanted it to. "No, thanks. I think two will work. I'll come home after church, change and grab something here to eat, but thanks for the offer. Then I'll just drive out."

"Sure. I would pick you up but if you prefer to drive, then come to the main entrance. You know where that is, right?"

"Yes, I've seen that big brick and black iron entrance a few times."

He rolled his eyes. "I don't know why I asked that. Of course, you have. My dad went a bit crazy when he made that entrance years ago."

"It's beautiful and from what I've heard is a great example of how large a ranch you're entering when you go through that stone and iron entry."

"Maybe so. Anyway, come through that amazing entrance." He grinned.

Genna's insides grinned, too. The man was amazing, with his tanned skin, enticing wide smile, and dark hair that, when he took his hat off, was slightly wavy and inviting to fingertips—*not* her fingertips, she reminded herself instantly. "Will do," she managed with just a curve of her lips, hoping her startling vision wasn't apparent in the sound of her voice.

"Good. So come up the lane and past the house, you'll see a few stables and a big red barn. I like red and this is a new one you won't miss. I'll be there waiting for you."

She smiled. "I'm looking forward to it. I'm ready to meet your cute little goats or kids. I'm envious."

"After you meet them, you might not be able to hold back and instead you'll jump back to wanting to bringing a load home with you."

He had a way with words she really liked, because

she really thought goats were adorable and he would see how much she thought so tomorrow. "I'll be there, and I can't wait. I'm glad I got to help you today. Really, I am. Even though I didn't cut anything up, I hope me carrying things did help. Wait, what about you going to finish tomorrow? Am I taking your day away?"

"They can put off putting the cattle in that pasture another day. I'll finish that job on Monday, so no worries. You have goats waiting on you, and I plan on introducing you." He flashed an amazing smile then headed toward his truck.

She remained where she stood as she watched him stride to his truck. *The man had a way about him.*

He climbed in and through the open window, he lifted his hand. "See you tomorrow. Have a good night."

She smiled. "You too." And then she watched as he backed the large truck out, then drove away, leaving a soft film of dust behind him. She stood there longer than she should have, watching that dust settle and his truck disappear out of view. She fought off a twinge of wishful thinking. Then she turned—spun, actually— trying to wipe that wishful thinking away with the wind from the rushed spin. She strode to the house, up the steps, and into the house. Only then did she realize she'd left the tray with coffee and cookies on it sitting on the outdoor table. She turned, headed out the door, down the steps again, strode over to the table, picked up the tray and carried it inside. She had work to do, and it had nothing whatsoever to do with thinking about West.

West Buckley was just a nice guy. That's it. She liked a nice guy, and that was where she drew the line in the dirt. No crossing over.

* * *

It was a great sunshiny day. As West strode from his truck to the red metal barn, he was glad how he had set up meeting Genna here instead of his house. He'd gone to church earlier and had been standing out on the front lawn talking with his brothers and some other men of the church when Genna had arrived. He'd tried not to be apparent in how much he appreciated seeing her in her pretty cantaloupe-toned dress that swished around her calves as she walked up in her pale gold-toned sandals with a slight heel to them. She looked gorgeous…and it had been hard to not stare.

Breathtaking, and that was what passed through his mind as she approached. His gaze had gone from her smile to her dark hair with that soft glistening of auburn in it. Then his gaze had flowed down her figure, all the way to her toes in those sandals; realizing what he'd been doing he yanked his gaze away and focused back on the men. He did not need anyone realizing that he was on his way to a thorough and deep infatuation.

Yep, infatuation. He wasn't going to call it anything more than that now because she sounded completely uninterested about that. And he couldn't let himself get carried away and run her away.

Now, as he entered the barn, he gathered up the feed he would need and carried it out to his truck. They had a few goats that roamed the main area of the ranch but the majority were raised at his favorite place on the ranch, the original home and barn where his grandparents had started the ranch. The place he now called home.

He had just had her come to the main house because

it was easier to get to and she could park her vehicle there and then ride with him to see the goats. He was tromping down a road he hoped wasn't terrible, but he wanted to see her reaction to his place. The place he loved most on this beautiful ranch he called home.

"What are you up to?" his brother Caleb called as he came out of a stallion's stall.

"I'm meeting Genna here. I'm taking her out to see the goats and their babies. She came out when I was over there near her cabin fixing the fence and well, I found out she really likes goats, babies especially, so I'm going to show her ours. She hadn't known we had them. So I'm taking her out there."

Caleb grinned big. The dude was always looking for fun and with the lights in his eyes, West knew he'd just given his brother something to explore.

"So she's coming out? That's great. Interesting, actually. Y'all going to have a good time?" He hitched a brow.

"Don't start that. She just wants to see some goats. That's all."

Caleb crossed his arms and cocked his right leg out

as he studied West. "I don't know, brother. I have a feeling that you've got your eyes on her. Me and Ryder were talking about it after me seeing your reaction when she walked into church today. And he then told me about y'alls lunch the other day. I'm wishing you good luck and a little fun. She seems like a nice person."

"She is a very nice person. And thanks for your good wishes, but please do not say something to her about your suspicions if she comes while you're here. She has a thing…about not getting interested in a guy. She's been done wrong."

"Really? Well, that sucks. All right, fine. I won't do anything you could get mad at me about. But I am going to wish you luck. She's a beautiful, nice lady and believe me, I've seen her watch you too so this could be great. Okay, I'm taking this horse out for a ride and I won't be here to get myself in trouble. So, see you later." He chuckled as he went back into the stall and led the saddled horse out and down the center aisle of the stables.

It was just like Caleb to ride every day. Even on days they weren't working, he loved to get on a horse and West was really glad he was riding out now. The sound of a car engine rode on the wind before they made it out of the stables. He picked up his pace and he saw Genna's vehicle as he walked out into the sunshine.

Caleb was ahead of him and lifted as he slid his boot into the stirrup and then settled in the saddle, he lifted his hand in hello. "Have a good time. West's goats are true entertainment." Then he shot West a grin as he urged his horse to a trot and headed toward open pastures.

Relieved Caleb was gone, West stopped at his truck and set the bag of feed in the back, then turned to smile at Genna as she closed the door of the car.

"Howdy," he said, trying to be playful. "Glad you made it."

Her pretty lips curved up as she looked at him. She wasn't wearing her cantaloupe-toned dress—he loved cantaloupes and missed it, but she still looked great. She had on a sleeveless sky-blue blouse with jeans and that pretty smile.

"I wouldn't have missed it, though I thought about it. I knew I had to come. I can't wait to meet the goats.

I see one over there." She pointed.

He turned in that direction and saw one of their adult billy goats as it roamed the pasture eating grass.

"Yeah, that's old Sergeant Two Toes. He likes to roam and be alone. He's one of those you can never know exactly what he's going to do, so we're going to let him have the pasture to himself and we'll go another way. We're going to load up in my truck, and I'm going to take you to where the majority of nice and friendly goats and babies are. Not the grumpy old billy goats."

"Oh, so y'all don't keep them here?"

"No. We keep them at my Gram and Gramp's original portion of the ranch. Actually, we keep them where I live. I keep that house going. Hope you don't mind going over there."

"No...that's fine. It'll be interesting to see where the ranch began. Where your grandparents lived."

He grinned. "I love it. I have to warn you though, that the red barn there doesn't look like this big red mountain of tin. It's original."

"Original? You mean like still what it was first made of?"

"Yes, it is. It's older, made of wood, though we put a metal roof on it to help sustain it. Yeah, even the red wood is hanging in there…well, with the care we, or me, give it. I enjoy keeping it healthy." He liked the way her smile grew at his word use.

"I'm intrigued." Her expression lit up. "I actually can't wait. I, well, you know, like I said, me and my parents traveled all over the world and I hardly remember where my past started. I saw my grandparents when I was small, but the memories of where they lived is foggy. And then we traveled and I would see them occasionally and have small memories. We didn't see them as often as I wished. So, I think it's really cool that you are keeping all this of your Gramp and Gram alive."

He did like this gal. She thought like him. "Then hop in and let's get going." He reached for the door but she had it open before he could and smiled as she hopped into the seat.

He chuckled. "You're quick."

"I try to be."

"So I can see that." He closed the door, then strode around to his and climbed in. "All right, here we go."

He put the truck in gear and headed toward the entrance of the ranch. Once at the end, he turned onto the paved road and drove until the main metal fence of the ranch ended at a dirt road, and then started up on the other side of the road. All of it was their ranch land but letting the dirt road have open passage until it connected at his house made easy access. He drove down the road that was bordered by the ranch fences, and then they reached the tunnel of trees.

"Oh, how beautiful," Genna exclaimed as the rows of large oak trees' green branches met each other and intertwined high over the road, nature making its tunnel.

"I've always enjoyed it."

They rounded a slight curve and another, then came out of the trees and then there, at the end of the open road, the mailbox painted with the Texas flag could be seen. The thick array of bluebonnets they always encouraged this time of year stretched up the drive to the old, huge red barn that you saw before you saw the white house.

"Goodness, I love it. Oh, West, no wonder you live out here. It has…it just has a feel of home."

The expression in her words tumbled through him. He loved it, and as he slowed the truck, he watched her. She had leaned forward, taking in everything about the place he loved. "Yeah, I asked Gramps before he died—I was still young and he was vibrant—if I could live in this house one day. And to my amazement, he left it in his will that this would be where I could live, if I still wanted to. I moved in the day after the funeral." He heard the emotion in his voice. He always got that way when he thought of Gramps and Gram, who died before his Gramps. He knew how much they'd loved this place and he did too.

Genna shifted so she faced him as they pulled through the gate. "That's so touching. I'm sure your Gramp knew you'd take care of it."

"Oh yeah, I always made it clear that that big red barn, as old as it was, would get treated, painted, updated and cared for, always trying to sustain its original appeal. As long as I'm alive, it will look as good as it can."

She looked back at the large three-story red barn with the lower level sides protruding on either side of the center entrance. "It's perfect."

"Gramp and his friends and relatives constructed that years ago. They all enjoyed helping each other with those big tasks, but this one was a whopper. He said it was a huge week of hard work and food, and then a celebration as all their families came and the party was thrown. He loved it, and Gram loved it, as did all those who helped."

Genna reached out, touched his wrist with her fingers, and squeezed gently. "That's wonderful."

He looked at her and her sparkling eyes and loved the fact she appreciated it. "I've kept it as much like he would have, although you'll notice it does have a little satellite sitting on the far back side. I tried to hide it as much as I could but it's there. My office is in there, and I have to have internet."

She laughed. "I see that little thing up there now that you pointed it out, but it's not too noticeable. But these days, completely understandable. You've done an amazing thing, but I have to say, I love the Texas flag mailbox. It goes with the look."

"Yeah, that wasn't something that started out all

those years ago, but it is something that Gramp did. When he saw it, he bought it and installed it. I'll have to eventually repaint it, since you can see the paint starting to peel. But it's held up and I like it."

"Me too. It's a great representation of this lovely place you're keeping up." She smiled and looked around as he drove down the dirt road that ran through the blooming bluebonnets and then through the gate leading into the yard of the barn.

He smiled as he pushed on the brakes, knowing what she was about to see, he watched her as she zeroed in on the goats.

The goats that had heard them approaching and were already running around the side of the barn to greet them.

"Oh, my goodness!" she exclaimed, delight in her voice. "You weren't lying. You have goats. *Lots* of goats and awe...sweet, adorable kids!"

CHAPTER SIX

Genna's heart exploded as she said the words watching as big and little goats race around the edge of the big red barn toward them. She laughed heartily when one jumped over the other one and then it did the same. The little kids were adorable, some solid colors and some spotted black and white or tan and white or all three colors. As she watched them, her attention was drawn to the barn again to see more coming their way.

She looked at a smiling West. "Oh my goodness, they are amazing. Can I get out?"

West chuckled. "Have at it. They are entertaining. And when we go in the back, you'll see even more."

"No kidding?" She laughed.

"No kidding about it. Those kids, all of them, are going to be happy to see you. And I'm going to enjoy watching them greet you. They are fun, and that's one reason I've always raised them here, just like Gramp and Grams used to do, the place is perfect with them. Grams had many stories about the acrobatics and fun those little and big goats can have. So come on, let's go."

"Awesome. I can't wait." Genna already had her door opened so now she stepped to the ground and pushed it shut behind her. Adorable couldn't even completely describe the romping excited animals hurrying to greet them.

She stepped forward, being careful not to scare them—if that were possible since they looked as if they were smiling and laughing as their little legs carried them across the large—huge yard. She didn't have to wait long as the two in the lead made it to her, hopping and kicking as they instantly snuggled up to her legs. Then one sprang up so its front hooves rested on her legs. The little cutie pie looked up at her and made a giggle-like sound as it took her in with its glowing eyes. The other one popped its front legs on the back of the other one so that it was closer to her, and it grinned up at her as it, too, made the giggle sound. It was wonderful, delightful, and everything she'd imagined from all the videos and pictures she'd looked at and enjoyed.

Unable to stop herself, she bent and there they were, both of them with front hooves on her thighs and happy little faces and sparkling eyes dancing. She rubbed her hands on each of their heads, and they accepted her touch excitedly. Their tails wagged and their bodies shook in rhythm. They were adorable. One was black with white spots on his black ears and a white streak wrapping around its belly and back. The other was golden tan, with white mixed in, like vanilla ice cream mingled with caramel. They were the same size and as she knelt there, petting them, more small ones reached her, a herd of babies and behind them a few larger ones, probably adolescents...teenagers.

The larger of them grinned and let out a loud drawn out, "Maa". The sound was funny, then all of them started with longer and both high and low noted versions. The sound was delightful, and she laughed, loving their sounds. In response, the smaller ones with the softer voices let out more short bleats. Instantly, as if being signaled, they *all* started sounding off together. She started laughing as she looked up at West and found him laughing, his eyes sparkling with enjoyment at her obvious delight. Suddenly, a larger goat popped up on its hind legs and slapped its front feet on her shoulders, startling her with its big lick to her jaw.

"Goodness!" She laughed as the goat sounded off a giggle as it tilted its head and studied her.

"Down, Jupiter." West laughed as he gently pulled the teenage goat from her shoulders. "They can get a little more active than you want. But he or any of them wouldn't hurt you. They just enjoy climbing. And wiggling their tails and rears."

As he spoke, one of the new ones jumped into the air, kicked his hind feet out, and squealed. And she just laughed as two of the small ones, still by her side, let out maa sounds, as if saying, "Go, go go." She couldn't help smiling and knew it was super huge as she looked back at West.

"I don't know how you can have these darlings out here and ever leave. I'd be playing with them all the time."

She rubbed their heads as they nudged their way closer and through the surrounding crowd to get notice from her. West chuckled as he reached down, and without asking if she was ready to stand up, he slipped his hands beneath her arms; he didn't hug her but lifted to help her rise to standing, and the goats slid off as she rose.

Grinning, he laughed, "Come on. I want to show you the yard, inside the gate. The playground and their favorite moving toys."

"Okay," she laughed too as she watched the little goats bouncing up and down as the larger goats seemed to know where they were going and led the way. Joy, delight, and elation fought inside of her for the emotions these sweet animals stirred inside of her. And she tried hard to not admit that feeling the touch of West's arms on her was part of those feelings raging through her. West kept one of his hands wrapped around her right bicep. She glanced down at his wide hand and tried not to show her delight in his touch.

"I'm hanging on because these little critters can get

so excited meeting someone new, and especially, it seems, you because you were so welcoming to them. Anyway, I'm going to hang on to you in case one of them happens to slam into your feet and sends you rolling. Hope you don't mind."

Oh, she needed to mind but she didn't. "Thanks. I'm having a blast. But you're right—I don't need to roll around on the ground with them."

They walked through the side gate into a fenced area that had more goats, some larger, and there on the side was a beautiful old white house, very well kept up but still not a recent build. The way the barn was situated and where he'd stopped the truck, she hadn't had a good view of it. If he'd pulled on up farther, she would have but he'd stopped as soon as she'd spotted the goats. It was a charming place. The long terrace had hanging flower baskets inbetween each porch post filled with red flowers that she believed were Ivy-Leaved Geraniums, which she loved. They hung a few feet above the wood porch railing making them impossible for goats to get to. There were three steps up from the rock path to the porch and a seating area with wicker chairs and a porch swing hanging from the ceiling with chains at the end. Charming. So very enticing.

She looked up at him. "Your house is wonderful. Just wonderful."

He threw his head back and laughed. "Yes, thanks. But honestly, I can't take any credit for the way it looks. I keep it like Gram always did, even the flowers. She loved those geraniums, that kind that works in hanging baskets. Couldn't have the kind in pots because the goats would chow down on them." He grinned when she grinned. "She raised them every year. Great memories come from sitting on those porch steps with those huge baskets of flowers overhead—she grew more than you see here, there were a lot of them. It was a happy feeling, sitting there with her. And Gramps would sit over there in one of the chairs, waiting for us to eventually go over and take the swing or the other chairs."

She studied him, loving the sound of adoration in his words. "That's so special."

He sighed softly. "It was. Gram and Gramps and all of it. And theses little fellas surrounding us help keep their ancestors alive in my mind and the memories of

Gram and Gramps. I enjoy all those memories and always will. If I'm sitting in the swing, which is where I enjoy sitting, the goats come up and nudge me or talk to me with their grunts and gargles." He smiled and she did too, as one of the goats did just that, as if knowing West was talking about him. "See?" He laughed and so did she, it was impossible not to.

"You've created a great playground out here."

"Yes, they enjoy it. I keep the young ones inside the fence most of the time and the cattle guard keeps them in. However, today, one of the bigger ones propped its feet on that railing beside the gate and got the latch open so that's how they got out to greet you. They don't run off usually, so it's not too worrisome. And you got a special welcome that you seemed to enjoy."

"I did." She had fallen in love with this storybook home and barn and the wonderful, acrobatic little goats running around in the yard, jumping, hopping, rolling, and kicking as they let their some soft and some loud voices be heard. They twitched their small tails, as if keeping a beat as they romped. She turned toward the yard, and for the first time looked toward the far corner of the barn and fence. And there stood two donkeys in front of several large yellow plastic barrels piled on top of each other as if bunkbeds. There were a few goats laying in them and watching the goings-on in the yard.

And on the top of the stack of barrels stood a large goat. It had thick horns and shaggy face hair, and was as balanced as he could be, standing up there watching as if he were king of the mountains.

"Look how he's standing all the way up there."

"They love to climb. The little ones can't make it to the top of those barrels yet but they want to and work at it. And over there—" He pointed at the gray donkeys. "Those are their favorite play toys." He laughed, such a charming and delighted sound as they watched the goats on the backs of them. And as some of the smaller goats surrounding them also saw them they raced to the donkeys and started jumping and trying to get to the donkeys' backs. Many were too small but there were others that made it and the dancing began.

"Oh my goodness. They actually let them do that." She watched one of the two jump across to the back of the second donkey. And the donkeys just stood there calmly as they let the goats use them for fun and then the others joined in and it was like a balance and knock off game. One on, two on, a third one knocked one off and it kept on and beneath it all the donkeys calmly stood. "This is amazing."

"Yep, I think so."

"And you get to sit on your porch and watch this every day?"

His sparkling eyes slammed into hers, sending delight radiating through her already escalating feelings of joy. "Not every day," he said, with a drawn-out sigh. "Because sometimes a cowboy has to work." He grinned, watching her. "But I feed them in the mornings and evenings and watch them showing off for me. Like they are doing for you now. I did this growing up and so did my brothers, and they still come for dinner sometimes and we laugh about it as we watch."

"Sounds great. And you sell them?"

"Yes, they would overpopulate if we didn't. I make sure they're good folks and are going to take care of them while the goats help take care of their yards and pastures with all the nibbling they do. And their kids romp and play with the goats. They love them. And I enjoy supplying them to the kids."

"I love it and now, more than anything, really want some." She paused as she petted the bunch now jumping around her. "But I know I work too much. But if they have others, maybe they don't totally need me. Right?"

He smiled. "Right. They need you when they're born, especially if, say, the mom has triplets, which can happen. And one of them is getting neglected and you have to step in and raise him. Do you see Dew Drop over there, the real white one with the black spot on her forehead?"

"Yes, she's beautiful. And I love her name."

He grinned. "I named her, so thanks. She's the third triplet of a group and was very small—thus the name. She got raised in the living room for the first few weeks. Then, when she was healthy enough, I moved her out to a pen, and then she got strong and is doing great. But it takes some extra time."

As if seeing them for the first time, one of the goats that had been playing with the donkeys now trotted to a stop in front of them. It lifted its head up, as if looking at the sky, and let out the cutest gurgling sound that she'd ever heard. Then it looked as if it winked at them before trotting over to West. He bent and gave the cutie a good rubbing between the ears and then its back. Both West and the goat looked completely happy.

Watching them, Genna's heart tightened, and she actually sighed with enchantment. "I think she loves you." And at her words, the thought she hadn't expected blasted through her: *like I could.*

No, she wasn't going there. *No, no, no…not at all.*

Absolutely not at all.

CHAPTER SEVEN

West looked up at Genna, her words digging into an area he wasn't sure had ever been dug into. But it felt great…wonderful. "I love her too. I basically saved her life and she's brought me a lot of joy. And, as you can see, I haven't let go of her. Dew Drop will grow old here with me. She reminds me of one my gram had when I was young. She's sweet and fun, very playful, but also likes finding things to do that don't just involve me." He laughed. "She had to learn that after she finally got well and able to be with the others like she needed to be. But I'll tell you, that little gal can climb those barrels over there and do a jig and loves every minute of it."

As if hearing him talk about her, Dew Drop let out a rampant squeal, spun and tromped almost on two feet over to the donkeys and sprang like an eagle taking off and landed lightly on the first one's back, then sprang the next. And then, like a graceful mountain climber, bounced onto the nearest barrel, then the next and the next, as if springing up four very fat stairs. When she reached the top one, the larger goat that had been standing watch let out a loud protest, as if saying, "This is mine—get down." But Dew Drop barely heard because she was concentrating on bouncing down the barrel stairs on the other side and back to the ground.

"Oh my word! She has to be worn out after that workout." Genna clasped her hands together beneath her chin and grinned at the now strutting goat.

He laughed. "Oh, she loves an audience. I have no idea why she waited this long to show off."

"I love it. And the donkeys just stood there, as if all that being jumped on didn't bother them."

"It's like God made them to be entertainment for these kiddos. Because he loved Gram so much, Gramps started this. He always had donkeys and goats—said they enjoyed playtime together. And so they have it all the time and it's entertaining." He watched her eyes, so lit up and telling him she was really enjoying this. "So I can tell you, it might be hard for you to keep up with them but if you decide you want some, I can set it up for you. But, in the meantime, you're always welcome to come over here and play with them. I'm here most weekends but I work full-time at the ranch, mostly handling the office stuff. But I do cheat and get out sometimes. Like fixing the fence." He paused, then it hit him. "You see those two chunky-looking ones over there?"

She followed his pointing finger. "Yes, I see them. Why?"

"They are expecting. And it won't be too long. I can call you when it's going to happen if you want to come over and welcome those babies into the world."

Her smile was emphatic. "I would love that. You really are tempting me terribly much, West Buckley. I mean, I sell clothes and you've got me wanting to raise little goats and sell them to people who'll really love and enjoy them."

He laughed, feeling the rumble inside his chest. "I have to tell you that I always thought you were great when you came to this town and started to bring more business to town for everyone with your website. You've been a real help to all the other store owners with that big online store of yours, and I guess an amazing following. Ruby and Josie Jane—they are thrilled, everyone is thrilled. You are a big asset to this town and...I..." *What was he doing?* "Well, I know that you really aren't looking to date or anything and I don't want to run you off because I like you being my friend— ignore that. I like being your friend."

She studied him, then reached down and rubbed the little goat that was nudging at her legs; she laughed when it licked her wrist but her eyes were still on him. "Thank you. I like you as my friend."

And there it was. She just wanted to be friends. But the truth was, he'd take her any way he could get her. So friends they were. And who knew? Maybe eventually she'd get over that creep who tore up her heart and maybe she'd see past him as a friend. He hoped so. One thing was for sure: he'd be here and he'd be her true friend.

"Well then, great. Would you like to come in and have something to drink or snack on? Or I've got supper in the oven—been cooking all day. We could eat and sit out here and watch them play."

"Well, I could…have a glass of ice water and sit on the porch and watch these animals play."

He smiled. "You've got it. And maybe after we sit there awhile, you'll decide you want to eat something."

"So what is it that you've been cooking *all* day?"

"A roast. It's simmering in the oven. It's Gram's recipe and Sunday tradition. So I've kept it up. Sometimes my brothers come over, and Mom and Dad if they happen to be in town. They all enjoy it. But today I didn't invite anyone because you were coming to see the kids out there playing and I thought maybe you'd enjoy testing out my gram's recipe. Roast and carrots and potatoes in gravy that'll make your heart sing and your stomach growl. I have to admit, I have her bread recipe but I'm not good at that, so I buy it in town. But it, too, is still good."

She laughed. "I tell you what—I had no idea you were this persuasive. Because now you've got my mouth watering and the sandwich I ate for lunch is already starting to suddenly disappear. I have to say, I want to try your gram's roast, carrots, potatoes. And I'll guess I'll make do with the store-bought rolls."

They both laughed at her words, and he realized he was still cupping her arm. He squeezed it gently, then ran his fingers down the back of her arm and then pulled them away. That wasn't exactly the move a friend would make but he certainly enjoyed it as he tucked his fingers in his pocket and then hung onto the feeling of her soft skin.

"Okay, then. You can come inside or wait out here for me on the porch and watch or play with the goats. But I promise you they will be out here when you come out."

"Then you have tempted me—I'll come inside. I want to see the house that these two wonderful people built. You bring them to life with your words."

His heart pounded. "I love my mom and dad but I have to admit my grandparents hold a serious place in my heart. So, come on, you'll enjoy it. I've added a few things. I mean, you know the world has modernized, and I have some of my own things but all in all, the feel is still there."

He was in there with them; their things intertwined really well and one day if he found someone to love and to love him back, he figured they'd mingle right in, adding their things among the memories. *She's standing right beside you.* His heart went on a rampage at the words racing through his mind.

He'd been admiring this beautiful woman the entire year since she'd moved to town. And he'd now promised to be her friend, so he could not overstep that boundary she had set.

* * *

She was in trouble, and she knew it. The man was enticing and so truly nice. Yes, he was enchanting. She didn't need to be thinking about that, but she couldn't help it. And the goats. Oh goodness, just thinking about all those cute animals outside the house and how much he cared for them and did it to honor his grandparents...it was just touching. And she knew she had to be careful because whether she wanted it or not, the man tempted her. Why else had she agreed to stay for dinner, even though she knew she needed to get out of there?

And now, walking into the living room, she saw the pictures hanging on the wall—a happy-looking, vibrant middle-aged couple she immediately knew was his grandparents. Of course, they'd aged but it was a wonderful picture to have hanging of them. It was like she could see West in them. And yes, she could see the other brothers in them, too. He was from a great family full of good-looking men. All single men. And she could tell much of those handsome looks came from the Gramp and his glistening emerald eyes, the same color as West's. The other brothers had varying tones of green, too.

When she followed him out of the living room and into the kitchen area, there sat a long, long wooden kitchen table with what…twelve chairs, she counted. And on the wall behind the table was a family picture. His Gram and Gramp and two men standing on either side of them, a pretty woman beside each of them. They were surrounded by a herd of smiling boys, ranging from what looked like less than ten years old to teenagers. She walked over to it. "This is a wonderful picture. So this is, of course, you and your brothers, and I'm thinking this couple are your parents."

He walked over. "Yes, so that's Mom and Dad. They travel a lot now, having a good time being free of the ranch this time of their lives. And then those two are my cousins and their mom and dad beside them. Not long after this picture was taken, they died in that plane crash and that's why it's still here. We all aged but they didn't. Hunter and Ace came to live with us and are practically brothers now instead of cousins. Anyway, I couldn't ever replace that picture because it has my aunt and uncle in it…it's got all of us. And though none of us were too terribly old there, Uncle Jed and Aunt Loretta will forever live in our memories. So, that's my basic family. And this table…actually, my gramps made it. He cut it, sanded it, and varnished it. I've revarnished it with him before he died. It's a sturdy table, and we had many meals here growing up."

She was touched by his love for his family, and her heart expanded. "They were wonderful, it sounds like, and you were very blessed to get to know them. And I can't believe you and your brothers didn't fight over this beautiful place."

He shrugged. "No, we didn't fight…I guess I was the first one who asked for it when they were living and after they died, I was the one he left it to in his will. My brothers are all great guys but they knew there was a special reason Gramps did that. They all love the ranch and love living on it but," he grinned, "it might be because Gramps knew I'd take care of Grams goats. It came as part of the deal." He laughed. "And that really could be it. There are a lot of goats out there and I love it. So I'm a rancher, a goat keeper, and the ranch office clerk—not sure if you know, I pay the bills—I'm a good calculator."

She laughed at his sense of humor and his downplaying of his part of the ranch business. "I'm sure you're great at what you do, and it seems like you do love the goats."

"True. And it gives my brothers the freedom to do what they want to on the ranch. Meanwhile, I feel privileged to do what I do and get to live here in this home."

She crossed her arms. "I love it. I think your gramp knew exactly what he was doing when he left it to you. I have a feeling he watched all of you closely and he knew that you weren't just telling him you wanted the place but in your actions you showed him you would take care of it. It's amazing. I mean, in all honesty, I saw your parents' home when I pulled in this afternoon. It's stunning, with all that beautiful stonework. But this is an amazing place in a different way. You'd fit in anywhere, but here seems perfect for you. And I have to laugh...I love the goats."

"Well, I'm glad you do..." They stared at each other. "Okay, well, let's get you something to drink." He turned and headed toward the refrigerator.

He grabbed them some tall glasses of water and when he handed the glass to her, their fingers brushed. Instant electric sparks shot through his to her entire body, with a jolt that singed its way through her. He nodded toward the porch and led the way. He sat on one end of the swing, giving her the option to sit on the swing and not be snuggled with him or to sit in one of the chairs. She knew he was giving her room, so she sat on her end of the swing, leaving the space between them.

Instantly, one of the small goats charged up the steps and raced to the swing, cocking his front feet between them, and looked from one to the other as he let out his babbling sound.

"Are they always entertaining?" She laughed.

"Always. But when it's time and they need to rest, they go in that back entrance where there is an area for them, or they climb up into the big barrels. They have options."

"Wonderful." She rubbed the little fella between the ears. Then he dropped back to the floor and raced back down the steps and out to play.

They were playing, romping and rolling, and it was addictive, actually. She could get used to this and she could, in her mind suddenly, see kids out there playing with the goats. She shut that thought down instantly. "Everyone sent out emails to all their customers and are getting responses, and so far they are great. People want to come. It's only been a day and when I looked at my phone earlier, the response has been huge. We're definitely having a town party in three weeks."

CHAPTER EIGHT

"Hey, why are you looking so happy this morning?" Zack asked him as soon as West walked into the stable.

West grinned at his brother, who was leading his horse from the stall. "It's okay for me to look happy. You got a thing against it?"

Zack chuckled as he placed a hand on his saddle horn and tugged, making sure it was tight enough. "No, I think it's good, seeing my brother almost dancing into the barn, your steps are so lightweight. What's up?"

West reached his hand up and scratched the nape of his neck below the back edge of his cowboy hat. *How did he answer this?* Should he be hiding that he was walking on air—nah, they would see it. He just had to make sure they knew he and Genna were friends. That beautiful woman he'd spent the day with, drinking their water and talking on the porch as they watched the goats romp and play. Then they'd gone inside and eaten roast and potatoes, and she had loved it. Even asked for his Gram's recipe, she'd liked it so much. The woman was just pretty perfect, as far as he was concerned. "Well, I just had a good day. You ever had a good day?"

Zack laughed as he stuck his boot into the stirrup. After he'd settled into the saddle, he looked at him. "Come on, you can tell me. Slack off all you want, but I have a feeling something happened yesterday afternoon. I heard a little rumor that you had a visitor out at the house."

"Did you hear that from Caleb?" That was the only person he knew who had seen them.

"Nope. If he knew, he didn't tell me. You know it's a small town and word travels fast. Actually, I overheard Josie Jane and Ruby talking at church. They were real excited that that pretty dress store owner was coming out to your house to see some goats. Is that true?"

He stared at him, then laughed. "Yeah, she came out to see the goats. She likes them, kind of has that in common with Gram."

"And you. You can't tell me you don't like them as much as Gram did. You do a good job out there, so I'm not complaining, and Gram would sure be happy to know how well you take care of them, raise them, and sell them to good homes."

"Yeah, you know I enjoy them. But yep, it's true Genna came out while I was working on the fence and helped me. And while we were talking, I found out she liked goats. So, I invited her out. They're out there, so why waste them on just me watching them?"

Zack laughed hard. "Yeah, that's right—why waste them. I think that's pretty cool." He lightly tapped the horse with his spurs and it walked out the barn doors, then stopped. "I wonder about when Gramp met Gram. She was raising those goats, and I guess he decided he liked them too, because he knew as much as she loved them, it was going to take him loving them too if he was going to win her heart."

West grinned hard at his brother's words. They were the truth. "Yep, that's how I think about it. And obviously they made a good match. We have this beautiful ranch, these cows and horses and amazingly fun, cute, romping goats. I can't have my first cup of coffee in the morning without watching them."

"That's why you're the perfect man to live out there. And you need the right woman to enjoy it as much as you do. Okay, I've got to ride. Being bent over struggling calves all day, giving them shots, is not the same as taking a ride. Been one of those kind of days and now, some quiet time." He lifted his hand and headed out.

All of them liked time out in the pasture alone. It had been Caleb the other day and today Zack. West liked to ride but he got just as much de-stressing sitting on the porch watching his goats romp around. He smiled as he went in the barn storeroom and picked up some extra bottles in case he needed them for the new goat or goats that would be arriving any day. And he was ready but hoped they came when he could call Genna, and she could be there with him.

That would make it perfect.

* * *

They had decided to wait until Tuesday after work for the store owners' meeting about the dance they were going to throw. They were meeting at Josie Jane's Wash and Repeat, where some could sit and have the group meeting. Everyone had had a chance to send out emails to all their clients and ask for responses, and they were going to talk about it. And as Genna closed her doors, dropped her keys in her purse, and walked across the street, she was pleased so many of the store owners beat her through the doors. They were excited. It just blew her away that she hadn't thought of this on her own and that it had taken one of her customers to give her this idea. It was brilliant and a way to help draw more visitors to town. And she was thankful her customer had brought it to her attention because it was just a very cool venture to explore.

She neared the door just as Jace, the feedstore owner's grandson, walked around the corner of the store with his large, happy dog that he held close to his side with the leash as soon as he saw her. Boulder, the large "Weim" liked to roll people over with his happy, zealous greeting of slamming his body into them for a hug. She halted, smiled big, and waited for them to reach her; then she wrapped both her free hands around him. Fun and cheerful was what the dog was to her. His big gray-blue eyes sparkled as his lagging tongue moved from one side of his mouth to the other, slinging out and trying to lick her wrist. She managed to dodge it with one wrist, but he got the other.

"Sit," Jace demanded and instantly the dog slapped his rear to the walkway and continued to grin.

He had her attention. "Hey sweetie, how you doin', Boulder? You're looking good, big fella."

Jace chuckled. "Yeah, I was just going to look in the window to see how many people were coming to the meeting. I'm not going since I have this big boy here with me but I'm sure whatever y'all decide will come out good. Gramps headed off fishing with Lew a few moments before I closed up, but you can tell them that he's in and he's got, well, you know, most of his customers are local, so he knows most of his clients are coming. So we're in and it should be fun."

She smiled at him. The good-looking cowboy loved to help his granddad and also run the ranch. He was a happy, recently married fella. "You tell him that we're excited about as many of your customers who want to come. I know they are young and old, married and single, and as crazy as it sounds, that's what started it. My customer wanted to bring her single daughter to my store and this town, hopefully to meet a cowboy. I'm not sure if she knows what her mother has planned for her when they show up for shopping and then a dance, too, but it will be interesting. It's not like anyone is going to have an instant love of someone, but it is inspiring."

Jace's grin was huge. "Yeah, but I can tell you from my own experience that dances are magical and it's cool that y'all are doing it. I mean, every person who came in had heard about it. Y'all came up with this on Saturday is what I heard, and it's traveled like fire. It should be fun. Exciting. Me and Lila are looking forward to it. She's in Austin working on a design with a large client. We think y'all are doing a good thing."

"Great. Well, I guess I better head in there. You can

peek in the window and I'll tell them what you said and they'll be happy. And I am too."

"Good thing. And I just want to tell you that it's great—how many people might have had a customer say that to them? They might have listened, then brushed it off and said, 'Nah, we're not going to do that.' But you, with the cool website you have and all those interested customers you've had coming here just to see your shop in our small town...well, it's awesome. And I think you need to know that. I'm not the only one who says that. It's a common, ongoing conversation around the coffeemaker in the feedstore. So, good job, our new Lone Star, Texas, resident. We're glad you adopted us."

She laughed, reached out and gave him a side hug. "I am too. I'm glad y'all adopted me. I can thank my mom for remembering it from when she came here as a girl and filling me with fun stories, and she always told me about it as we traveled all over the stinkin' world. I so longed for a place to belong. And then, well, I was nothing but embraced and it's a wonderful feeling. So let's do this. Who knows? Maybe we'll embrace someone else who needed just what I needed when I came here. I'm excited."

He grinned and gave her a nod as he pulled Boulder back, who was trying to stand on his hind legs and give her a hug since he'd seen her give Jace a hug. The dog was amazing. But right now she didn't need to take on the weight of his big, tall body and his long arms on her shoulders as he enjoyed a hug.

Jace pulled him away and they headed back the way they'd come. Boulder kept looking back over his shoulder at her, and she could see in his eyes that oh, he wished he could stay. She adored that dog.

She opened the door and walked inside, smiling at the crowd—this was going to be good.

"There she is," Josie Jane called from where she stood among the large circle of chairs that the storekeeper had at the center of her store for friend gatherings or customers who just wanted to sit for a few minutes before starting shopping again. Or a really tired husband or wife whose mate was on the shopping spree and they needed to sit down. It was a big enough store that it handled it really well. And Ruby from the diner loved to take time when she had it to come over, and she and Josie Jane would figure out all kinds of things that were going on in town or needed to happen. Now they were on fire about this idea that her customer had had, and they were going to bring it to life. *So cool.*

"Hey, everybody. I'm so thrilled by the turnout for this."

"We are too, pretty gal," Lumas Camry said, an older man, who owned the New and Antique Field and Stream Supplies just off Main Street, about midway through town. He had all kinds of supplies, antique and new. He'd supply anyone with what they wanted, from working in their gardens to fishing in their lakes and even the ocean. The man loved what he did and was also a good friend of Jace's grandfather Bo and his friend Lew, who loved to fish. "This is a great idea, and my customers were thrilled. You can't believe how many of them who are married with kids, mostly adult kids, were thrilled with the idea. So, anyway, I've got at least thirty replies, so that's about sixty or more planning to be here. This is just the first actual day of replies, so there will be more."

"And I'm the same way," Beatrice Ratcliff said

from her seat in the comfortable blue checkered chair, where she had her crochet needles out, just working away. Beatrice owned the knitting shop three doors down. Many of the people who came to town looking for secondhand things for their home loved to buy knitting supplies, too. Beatrice was rich and didn't need the money; she just enjoyed what she did and that was pretty cool.

"That's wonderful. So did you have any replies to your messages?"

Beatrice's face filled with a wide smile and it made everyone in the room chuckle as her soft green eyes sparkled and she leaned her short, white-haired head to the side. "Of course I did. Do you know how many of my customers are wanting to bring their kids home, single and married—well, not home with them—but here to have a good time? It's like they just want to embrace our little town, and I'm excited to be involved. Who knows—maybe one of my grandkids will come— and maybe fall in love. Now that would be a miracle for me. I miss not seeing them much more than twice, maybe three times a year. But they are busy and I understand."

Millie, owner of the antique store across the street, with her short red hair and lanky arms, smiled from where she leaned against the counter with her nonstop legs tucked into her bright-red boots. She was a hard worker, with a great business. "I like this idea, and I sent out over a hundred and fifty emails and more than two-thirds of them replied almost instantly. They are excited so just tell me, if I have that many people coming and all of y'all have all your people coming, what in the world are we going to do? This place is going to be packed. That little community center isn't going to hold everybody. Now, I'm not saying we can't do it, because I'm excited and ready to put on a show. I just want to know the plan."

Everybody laughed at her enthusiasm.

"Now, now, now." Josie Jane beat Genna to the answer. "We already thought that out. We're going to have a street dance. Don't you think that'll be wonderful? We can string up lights, have a street dance with an awesome band with big loudspeakers that promote the sound. We can just party all down Main

Street. However, many people who want to come can come. Of course, that means we all have to cook some good things to eat. But I know all of y'all like to cook…especially you, Millie."

That brought on more laughter because everyone knew Millie hated to cook.

Millie grinned but sent Josie Jane a warning look. "I might not cook but I can sure carry chairs and put up lights. If a man can do it, I can do it."

All the men grinned back at her because they knew it was true.

"That'll be wonderful," Genna said. "You know we can't do without you." She really enjoyed this enthusiastic woman. She was just three doors down from her, and she'd stop in every once in a while and look at all of Genna's clothes. But she'd never taken any away with her. This woman liked her blue jeans, her red boots, and whatever shirt she picked out—usually a Western shirt. Nice and neatly ironed, tucked in to expose a very large belt buckle she'd won when she competed in women's barrel racing. She was wonderful, a great contributor to this community. "You're going to be a huge help, and I love your enthusiasm, and your customers'. Goodness, their response is wonderful."

And then it started; all the others started calling out the numbers of their customers who were coming, as if they weren't going to be beat by Millie. And that was even more exciting. When everyone stopped calling out numbers, they didn't even have time to calculate them, they were flying across the room so fast. But one thing for sure was it was going to be one great street dance. An enthusiastic street dance.

But what thrilled her most was how thrilled they were about it. "Y'all, this is exciting. I mean, goodness, I'm sorry it had to be one of my customers who brought this idea to our attention. We are going to have a blast, and our customers are too. And I know we don't have a lot of bed-and-breakfasts around here, but if we did, this shows that this place might be packed. So here is a thought. Maybe we need to pray that a few people want to come to town and open some B&Bs if they see how much fun people are having. Just think of the advertising we could do. It is an amazing idea…matter of fact, I live in a little cabin out there on that huge ranch all those handsome Buckley men own and work, but I might just think about opening my own B&B. Even if I don't live there, I could have someone to oversee it. I love my shop so I'll be working there. Boy, my brain is now working nonstop with this new idea."

And it was on a rampage. She had the money, so she knew she was about to start looking for real estate to invest in.

Ruby, who sat in one of the chairs in the far corner, grinned. "I think that is a fantastic idea. I can see our already busy stores get even busier if they come and spend the night instead of having to travel to other towns. Who knows, when I talk to Red about it, he might want to buy a big house for visitors. Even if it's a flub, we need the money for a tax write-off. Then again, we have a cabin on our place. We could start with that—I might even put that up for rent in time for the dance. I'll have to clean it up some. No one has stayed in it for a long time. But it is really cute. Brilliant idea."

Leroy, who owned the store along this street, chimed in. "I hope Red likes that idea. He stays busy cooking and might not like having to fix up a cabin."

"Don't you worry. If I start it, I'll take care of it. And I know the one thing this town has to have is him cooking, so I won't be doing anything that distracts him. His cooking brings people back just because it's so good."

Little tiny Arabella Samuels, who owned the small bakery at the end of Main Street that had been open all of her adult life, smiled, rather weakly, but she looked happy. "I'll tell y'all the truth. I'm about ready to retire and I may have to go ahead and put it on the market with all these people y'all are going to bring to town. Someone may want to buy it. So up for sale it's going, and I'm going to start ads in the newspapers. Who knows, I might bring a new baker to town. You know, my place is cute and it does have history and with what we're doing, history is important."

Josie Jane sprang to her feet and stared at Arabella. "That is a wonderful idea. I know you've been ready to retire. So soon, maybe, you'll be able to come sit in here with me during the day. Who knows, at the dance maybe one of the single women will be interested, buy it and then marry one of our cowboys."

"I hadn't thought about that," Leroy said. Then his eyes lit up. "And you know what—my old buddy Johnny Foster who moved away a few years back recently passed away from that darn cancer that was after him and left his pretty three-story house out on Rocky Road to his granddaughter, Sydney. Now that place would make a great bed-and-breakfast, if any of you want to contact her and see if she'd want to sell it."

Ruby looked at him so sweetly. "I'm so sorry about Johnny. We miss seeing you and him roaming around together and eating breakfast together at the diner. He was a nice fella. I hadn't heard he'd lost that battle, but I'm so glad he was with his family when it happened. And that place is wonderful. Y'all, he would love the idea of his house being a place for people to come and enjoy this town. I may check in with that sweet Sydney. She loved her grandfather and used to come visit, but at her age, with college and then work, I'm sure coming out here was hard. Another reason him moving to Wichita Falls to be with them was a good thing. He loved his family."

Leroy nodded in agreement. "Yes, he did. But yeah,

check into that, Ruby. Maybe little Sydney would want to sell it, knowing why you want it."

And then everyone started talking about everything that had been brought up and Genna just stood there, listening to all the chatter. The happiness in the room was so moving, and she was glad she was here in this sweet town. It delighted her to see the exhilaration in the room. She couldn't wait to see what could come.

What could come? In her head, without even willing it to, West's handsome face flashed before her and all those adorable, darling goats and her day that she'd spent there. She had thought about him so much since Sunday, and he'd promised he'd be as helpful as she needed him to be. And his brothers too. She liked that because just like Josie Jane had said when they'd first discussed it, the cowboys had to draw some attention. Not that she was interested in getting married. *Nooo, it didn't*. How many times she'd thought of West during the day was not something she was ready to get into.

Look at what she'd started—the hope and happiness she was bringing to this town. The last thing she wanted to do was risk messing up. Giving her attention and her heart to someone, then it falling apart and then here she'd be stuck, in a little town that she loved, heartbroken from a man who didn't want her— oh, no...that was not happening. She was not going down like that. As she stood there, West's handsome face hopped right back into her thoughts, and she gently pushed it away.

Gently—she couldn't be rough with him, but she did push him out of her thoughts. Falling in love was not something she planned to do.

But yes, he was a friend, and he had said he would be. And that was where he would stay.

CHAPTER NINE

On Thursday morning, West walked into the barn where they had a coffee area set up for where they could meet or wait for a horse to be born or a calf to be born. It was a great place and had come in handy many times over the years. Sometimes it was a resting spot after riding wild horses but today it was for something different than any other of those times. Today it was to talk about the upcoming event that had the whole town in an uproar of excitement. He had eaten breakfast at the diner this morning, and it was buzzing with enthusiasm. He'd never seen the townsfolk so motivated, and it was all due to that beautiful Genna and her brilliant idea.

Yes, she gave credit to the woman customer who asked her to hold a dance so she could try to fix up her daughter but Genna could have easily closed the door on that. Instead, her brilliant mind had gone to this and he had never, ever in all of his life, seen such excitement. His brothers hadn't either and as they came in and sat down with a cup of coffee, a glass of water, or a soda, they all looked at him and grinned.

He grinned right back at them. "So are y'alls heads swimming like mine about how excited this town is about this gathering?"

Ryder held his cup of coffee up in salute. "I tell ya. I've got to raise a cup of hot coffee to that gal. This is an amazing idea. Not that I'm looking to find someone to marry and fall in love with or anything, but you all know I love to dance. So yay, bring it on. I hope there's a lot of excited gals who want to dance with me." He took a drink of his coffee as everybody laughed because they knew Ryder Buckley, their oldest brother, who was probably at the age of someone who should be thinking about finding someone to settle down with, was not interested.

Nope, the guy liked being single, and he might just stay that way. They also knew their mom and dad were hoping someday soon he—or any of them—would get married and give them a grandchild. And that was something that Ryder was not interested in. No way. And he had made that perfectly clear. But West couldn't help but wonder whether it would be that way. Ryder had his funny ways but he was a great guy and the women loved him. And all of the single women in town, the few there were, all had gotten hold of him and knew he was not available. He was just a great dancer and he enjoyed dancing, and that was what the gals loved about him. If they weren't interested in falling in love, then he was the perfect one to dance with and not worry about getting someone's interest peaked because he wasn't interested at all.

Dustin grinned and West knew he was thinking probably the same things about their brother that he'd been thinking. "Well, I'm not going to go and be that blunt about it but yeah, I'm looking forward to it. I haven't danced with anyone new in a while. It's hard finding someone to date, we work so many long hours and would have to drive to find someone so I think it will be fun. Getting to know someone, even if it is just for an evening, sounds fun. The idea that this could become something we do more than once or twice a year, or maybe more than four times a year, is exciting. This little town could get known for that. I'm in—not that I'm looking to fall for the first girl I ask to dance at the party, but I'm not going to shut my door to it." His gaze went straight to Zack, who they all had witnessed slamming the door on love and hadn't shown any signs of opening it to look for love after he'd been dropped by his first love.

Zack met his gaze. "Yeah, you make fun of me as much as you want to. I know what I'm doing, and this is exciting because I will enjoy watching you guys get married. But don't go making fun of me because I feel the way I feel. Until you've had your—well, I'm not going to say my heart is broken, because I'm long over that part. But, until you've had your…hmmm, what's the words I want to use…your guardrails busted, don't you be laughing at me, because you just don't know. And I'm hoping that none of you go through that fiasco, 'Cuz it just doesn't feel good." He stared them down.

"I wasn't trying to be mean," Dustin said.

Zack nodded. "I know, but, this sounds fun and I

might, actually—*might*—dance with someone. I'm not promising it but, I will enjoy watching you guys have fun, watching y'all dance and listening to everybody talk about it. Because let me tell you, when everyone is out there dancing, there is a bunch of talk going on among all the older folks in town. And with new faces coming in, believe me, it is going to be alive with chatter. It's going to make me grin, make me laugh, and have something to tell y'all when you stop having your evening of fun."

Everybody laughed because it was true; they knew that the town of wonderful older people were going to be watching. And maybe talking. They remembered the last dance when Jace and Lila had gotten together and Zack, Jace's best friend, had been just as excited as everyone that those two had finally had a happy ever after. Because now they were doing great. West knew that Jace was probably enjoying watching what was going on, like they all were. And he knew his brother was probably going to hear from Jace about these dances. Zack hadn't promised anything to anyone but had made it clear that he was not putting himself in that position ever again.

Ace, their cousin, leaned against the counter beside the coffeepot, holding his cup of coffee as he watched them. "Well, I'm coming and I'm not guaranteeing anything, but it should be fun."

Hunter, who sat in the chair closest to his look-alike twin brother, snatched his hat off and raked his hand through his curling hair. "Well, I can just tell you that I'm going to be watching. I mean, I don't know about me, but I think it would be fun to watch any one of you fellas have an enjoyable night at the dance. And maybe, just maybe—I know my mom and dad, if they were here, would be hoping me and Ace would get married and give them some grandbabies. At least I think they would. We were only ten when we lost them but I know they loved us so much that they'd want more of us and are probably up in heaven, getting excited that we're the age where that could happen." He held his hand up. "But we're probably not going to be the first to find love..." He grinned. "We're the babies in the group, while several of you are about to be too old for love—so you better get busy." He laughed, and they did too.

West grinned, enjoying his cousin's way of looking at things. He knew his mom and dad were excited about it. They'd been traveling and enjoying themselves and had a cruise trip planned but canceled it when they heard about the town event and were headed this way. They were thrilled, and he knew it was probably because they were hoping one of their sons would find love, maybe at a dance, and then they'd get some grandbabies somewhere soon in their future.

"Y'all do know that we're going to help set up that night. So be ready to put up sparkling lights and to be of aid with carrying things around, planting flowers...whatever they need, we're available to help. Yes, I know we have work but I figured we can stop what we're doing and assist when needed. Maybe take turns if we're too busy. Some of the other ranches are going to do it too. We've got a lot of cowboys around here and no reason all those older folks have to get out there and overwork, trying to help the town have a fun night. We're going to take care of them. Does that sound okay, sound good?"

All of his brothers were smiling and some laughing

as they raised their coffee mugs, water glasses, and cans of soda.

"We're in."

"Yeah, we're in," was the echo going around the room.

He liked that his brothers and cousins were in on it with him. Because it was going to be fun. And he could not stop thinking about how going to town a lot to assist would put him in position to see Genna again. Truth was, that since she'd come out to the ranch and seen his place and all his cute goats, she had kind of disappeared. When he was at the diner, she hadn't come in for breakfast or lunch. He hadn't seen her cross the street even—well, one time she had and his hopes that she'd come in the diner had surged but nope, she hadn't come in. She just stayed in her dress store. So, maybe, he'd see her.

He'd promised her they were just friends and that's what he would be, so he hadn't gone in her shop to ask her what was up. He just planned to be there, helping out getting ready for the party and hoped he'd see her. And maybe if he helped her put some lights up, their hands would touch and he'd feel that electric volt rage through him like he'd felt before. Or even just meet that beautiful gaze of hers, that also shot him full of bolts of lightning. He sure liked it, but he'd promised her that if she just wanted him as a friend, that was what they'd be. He'd just pray that one day she might want more, and if she ever did decide she wanted more, it would be with him. Not with some fella she met at one of these dances and her heart changed.

His heart hurt at the thought for a moment but he had to deal with his brothers, so he focused on them. He grinned. "Okay, so we have a party to get ready for. And if you hear of someone who needs help who hasn't gotten to me, just let me know or jump in and do it. Just know we're all here to assist in any way we can so let everyone know if they need us, we're ready."

"It sounds good," Ryder said, then lifted his coffee again. "Okay, fellas, let's get busy. The ranch is calling our name. Can you hear all the mooing going on? It's time to get busy."

Everyone got up and headed for their trucks that were already loaded with saddle horses. They were heading to one of the far pastures of the ranch for some rounding up. West sometimes didn't go if they had a cattle or horse sale coming and he had to prepare for it, but this month he was pretty caught up on all the office work so he decided to go. He needed something to take his mind off Genna and wondering why she was avoiding him.

CHAPTER TEN

"That looks great." Genna stood beside the ladder and looked up at the lights stretching across the road from Josie Jane's to hers, and then looked as it zigzagged all down the street. They'd crisscrossed at least twenty feet down the middle of town, maybe thirty feet, giving them lots of room for a fun dance night beneath the lights that were sparkling on and off. And then, outside the lights, would be tables of goodies to enjoy and drinks. It was going to be fun and she couldn't wait.

She looked up at West. *Goodness, the man was so gorgeous*. And though she'd tried to avoid him all of last week, she hadn't been able to turn him away when he'd come over earlier and asked to help her. She'd watched him and his brothers helping others all day with anything and everything they needed. So, when he'd come over to her, she'd been unable to not accept his offer. It had been hard on her, trying to avoid him, and now, she looked up at him in his boots and jeans and body-clinging T-shirt that emphasized his toned muscles as he'd streamed the lights above her.

"Glad you think so," he said drawing her gaze from his chest to his grin.

She realized those emerald eyes of his were drilling into her, and she couldn't think of what she might say next.

"Well, I guess I," he continued after the blank spot of no words from her. "I better climb down and do whatever else you want me to do."

His words were drawled out in that Texas tone she loved. It rang through her, like a slow rhythm country song and sent her heart fluttering. She had not stopped thinking about this man all week. This man and the sound of his voice, the appeal of his beautiful eyes, his loving attitude, his wonderful goats—that she so wanted to see—yes, this man was special. He had told her he felt like tonight might be the night the baby goats would be born. He'd invited her to come to the house and be ready to welcome them into the world, if he was right.

Oh, how she wanted to do that. He'd told her the babies were late and he didn't think the mama could carry them any longer. It would either be naturally tonight or tomorrow a trip to the vet.

"Well, I think we've almost got it done," she said at last, focusing on the event and not him. "We're going to be ready a whole week before the event. But I love it. And thank you for coming and helping. I probably could have gotten it done but to be honest, I enjoyed you being here helping me." Her blurted words echoed through her, but they were out and no taking them back so she quickly added, "And all of your brothers and your cousins have been wonderful; everyone has said so. And you can tell by the happy looks that are everywhere. Even tall, lean, do-it-her-way Millie Watts has enjoyed watching you and your brothers and the other cowboys climbing up those ladders." She laughed because she had seen exactly what she'd said.

He laughed too. "You know, my dad said that when they were all younger, Millie was a go-getter in the rodeo and that there were many fellas who grew up with her who would have fallen in love easily if she'd have just given them a little bit of a chance."

"Really, why didn't she?" she asked, understanding the rodeo buckle now.

"As someone who was focused on becoming a rodeo top champion in barrel racing, she hadn't focused on anything but that. And she'd made it too. And along the way, she'd fallen in love with one of her rodeo buddies, a bull rider, and they got married while they were out there, hopping from one rodeo to the other. Then he got killed on the bull and she quit at the top of her game and came home. It was all sad, and though she still wears that buckle you've seen her wearing, nobody believes she's ever been on a horse again. Not to run those barrels she so loved or even to ride in the pasture for pleasure."

"Oh how sad."

"Yeah, it is. She'll talk about it and reminisce but it's like when she lost him, she just shut down that side of her life, came home and opened that store. And like no horse riding, no one thinks she's ever looked at another fella either. But she seems to enjoy herself in her new way of life, she just has guards up I think."

Genna's heart pounded rapidly against her rib cage as she thought about that tall, smiling woman who was determined to do most everything on her own. And the loss of love she must have suffered when her bull-riding cowboy lost his dream—and her—the night he died. Her eyes teared up, thinking about it.

"I didn't mean to make you cry." West placed a hand on her arm.

Tingles shot through her at his touch, and oh, how she'd missed that. Longed for it. The thought of poor Millie and what she must have suffered hit hard. Genna looked at West, blinked trying to clear the tears. "I don't mean to cry. It's just so sad. You know, she…did what she loved and found the man who did what he loved, and they were great in the moments they were married. And then she lost him so quickly. You know, it takes some people a lifetime to find the person they want to live with and love forever." Her words trembled. "And, for them to be taken away so quickly—it just hurts."

She thought about herself, she didn't lose the man

she loved; no, she'd been thrown away by the man she'd thought she loved. Thankfully she'd come to know she didn't love him and the reality was he'd done her a favor by breaking it off. But still, standing there, looking into West's wonderful eyes, she thought about poor Millie, who had lost the man she'd loved so quickly, and she'd evidently never thought of dating anyone else. But, there was a difference, she realized.

A big, huge difference.

Millie had felt that love, had known that deep, true love, and enjoyed it for maybe just a short time, but she'd had it. And that was something Genna was fighting not to do.

She swiped her tears from her cheeks and yanked her gaze away from West's penetrating gaze. Digging, searching eyes. *Had he seen what she suddenly knew was true?*

She loved West.

How had that happened?

She just barely knew the man. Unable to stop herself, she spun and strode down the street, away from everyone.

What was she doing? What was she thinking? How had she let this happen?

Suddenly, his hand was on her arm again, tugging her to a halt. "Genna, wait. What's wrong?"

Breathing heavily, she turned slowly and looked up into his eyes. He was just a few inches from her, and there were those eyes, concern illuminating from them. She just stared at him, and then, as she stood there, he lifted his palm and cupped her cheek.

Lightning shot through her. "No," she gasped softly.

"Please tell me what's wrong," he said, his fingers warm against her skin. "You look so sad. I can't stand it. Genna, I need to know what's hurting you. What's keeping you from stepping out and seeing what's between the two of us? You've pulled away after our...what I thought was a great afternoon at my ranch house."

Her lip trembled and her gaze dropped to his tempting lips. She had woken up several nights, wondering what his lips would feel like. She tore her gaze away and stared at the ground, taking in their boots that were straddling each other. His, hers; his, hers.

He stepped closer and she shivered.

"I'm scared," she blurted, still staring down. "That's what's wrong."

His fingertips slipped so they could lift her chin, and their eyes met. "Please don't be scared. Come to the house tonight. Just come out and enjoy watching the mama goat give birth to her babies. Just stop thinking about whatever is holding you back and give us a chance. Because, I have to tell you, I care for you, Genna. And I wasn't really expecting that. It happened so quickly but I'm not a guy who would mess up what is as special as what I feel is between us."

She stared into those eyes of his and thought about the eyes of the one who'd messed her up on thinking about love and commitment. The one she knew West wasn't like at all—but could she step out again? Here in this town she loved, here where she loved the townsfolk and the atmosphere and always wanted to be a part of it…could she risk that?

He didn't say anything else as they held gazes but he nodded, as if encouraging her to say yes.

And then, before she knew what she was doing, she nodded too. "Okay. I'll be there."

* * *

The moment five o'clock hit, Josie Jane grabbed her purse and headed for the door. She'd been able to decorate a little outside while checking in on customers who were looking at things in her store. She'd enjoyed watching what was going on outside and had told customers to just give her a wave if they needed her inside. She'd also given each of them details about what was going on outside in case they wanted to come.

Now, as she walked out onto the walkway she was delighted because everything was looking delightful. The lights strung across the streets and the decorations along the sidewalks, flowers and lights in the windows...all beautiful. It was going to be a fun dance and everyone looked happy, getting ready for it.

But a certain couple had her alert signal flashing.

She locked her door and turned toward the street and spotted Ruby hustling toward her. Poor Ruby hadn't been able to help today because they'd been extremely busy and even with the new help they had, she was still needed. Especially considering everyone visiting in town wanted to eat there, and then all those working on decorations needed to eat too. Maybe now that it was a little in-between mealtimes, they'd slowed down and Ruby was free because here she came.

"Ruby, slow down or you're going to trip and roll."

Ruby waved her hand and laughed as she reached the sidewalk. "I'm getting a break. Come on. Hurry. We need to go."

"What do you mean? Where are we going?"

"I called the owner of the house—you know, the granddaughter who inherited it when Johnny Foster passed away. And she is thinking about moving here, but it's iffy. She said I could walk around and look at it if I wanted to but she couldn't promise anything."

"What do you want her to promise? Wait, are you wanting to buy that big place?"

"I would love to buy it, but she said she was trying to decide whether to move here since thinking of selling it is hard for her. But still, I haven't really looked at the place in a long time, and suddenly I have the urge to walk around it and imagine its potential."

Josie Jane liked the idea very much. "Then hop in and let's go."

On the same track they climbed into her car and she backed out carefully. Everyone was finished standing on ladders in the middle of the road but she just wanted to be careful.

"So, did you see them today?" Ruby asked.

Josie Jane looked over at her friend, who had a coy look in her eyes. "Are you talking about West and Genna?"

"Yes. Exactly. I just happened to be at the front window, waiting on some of the tables there, and saw him over there helping her with her lights. And then she spun away and stalked down the road, her hips swinging and her hair dancing with the firm-footed steps she took. Then he hurried to catch up to her and wrapped his hand around her arm and gently stopped her. She turned back, and you should have seen the emotion on her face. I guarantee you that something is going on between them."

"Yes, it's obvious. I was standing out front of my shop and was watching them when that happened. Something *is* defiantly going on."

They both grinned at each other and then Josie Jane concentrated on turning at the intersection of Main Street and Elm. The town was small but there were neighborhoods with pretty homes kept up over the years and some that were aging. It was a normal small town. And most people lived in the surrounding countryside. Elm Street ran straight and had small, older homes on it, then a curve over a small bridge and they had just a little way to go to another curve, and there the house would be.

"Did you see how Millie was enjoying having all those cowboys helping her?" Josie Jane asked.

"No, I didn't see that. I couldn't stand in the window the whole time. What happened?"

"Well, you know how she is so set on living alone. You know, I can't say anything because I'm not ever going to remarry, so I can't judge her but she is a little younger than us, and she's been single most of her life. But, I just look at her and think she could be happy if she'd let herself fall in love again. I mean, she didn't have a long-living love like I had. Like I was blessed with, or what you're having with Red. She just had that short life of marriage that ended in such a tragedy, with him being hung up underneath that bull and trampled. That terrifies me whenever anyone wants to do that, but if they love it, they do it. And she always says, he was doing what he loved when he died, so she can't regret it. As she says, it was his time. Anyway, I just can't not think that she could find happiness again and know what it feels like to live a good life, longer than a year with that love. I did it and you're still blessed with it. So I just keep hoping that that woman would one day find love again."

Ruby turned a little in her seat belt and drew Josie Jane's gaze from the road momentarily. "I am with you on that. She is just living her life like it's wonderful, and it is. She enjoys her store but you're right; her love ended so quickly that I'd be thrilled if she got to experience that happiness again. I wonder if there is someone out there for her and he just hasn't come into her life yet."

Josie Jane was looking at the road again as they rounded the curve. "I agree. Do you think there is someone here in town for her?"

"Well, maybe. But you know there are a lot of men in town who do watch her constantly. Several of them, actually."

"Well, yes." Josie Jane had noticed that. "I know that. She dances with them sometimes at our townsfolk dances but I haven't ever seen sparks flying around. So if there is something brewing, it's really on a low flame."

"Right, exactly. If one of those guys has her on his heart, then it's really not showing. And same for her— really hidden, dug down deep with cement on top of it, hidden. Oh, there's the house."

Josie Jane was focused on it as she turned the car and drove down the tree-lined drive that led to the large house. It was a very pretty place but could easily be forgotten back behind the trees that needed trimming and the yard that needed attention. It was evident that none of the owners had been there in a while. But as they drew close to the house, it was just a big, beautiful house: white wood with a large front porch and three large stories. A wide house that had many bedrooms in it; if she remembered right, there were two, maybe three bedrooms on the first floor, with the large kitchen and living room and back room that was a family room. It had a view of the backyard that had once had a large rose garden in it. Then she was pretty sure there were four bedrooms on the second floor and at least two on the top floor. It was a giant house built after their first one burned down. They'd made money in ranching and oil as it was first being discovered. "To think how much land this man owned, and he sold it all to the Buckleys but this small acreage that surrounds this house."

"Yes, but he kept the oil rights, and I bet all those children and grandchildren—not sure how many grandchildren he has other than the granddaughter, but they have plenty. And obviously enjoy the city life instead of our country life."

Josie Jane parked the car and stared. "This would be an awesome B&B. You're absolutely right. It's right here next to town and such a great size."

"This was meant to be a bed-and-breakfast," Ruby

said.

"It looks like it. But it's not a call for us to make." Josie Jane opened her car door and Ruby did, too; they both stepped out and headed to the house.

They walked around, studying the place, looking in the windows and imagining its potential.

"It's perfect," Josie Jane said, in total awe now that she had the picture of what this could be in her head. "It might need a little upgrading but it wouldn't need much updating as far as I can see from outside view."

"I agree. And I'd love to put some money into it. But looking at it now, I guess I hadn't realized just how big it is. We go out the other side of town, so I don't come by here often. But it's within walking distance or bike riding and of course a drive from town. And it has a view of the pastures and yet if they decided they want to sell it, they could ask and get a lot of money for this house. I don't know if I'd be wanting to go that deep into it, and I can tell you Red wouldn't. He has enough on his hands. And if the town were to grow and get busier, he won't have time or want to have something else on our shoulders. So it's not for me as much as I'd thought it might be."

"I totally understand. You have a lot on your plate already and good food is a must. So keep your attention there. Genna said she was toying with this idea. But she's probably not thinking about one this big either."

"Probably not."

Josie Jane nodded. "For me either. So who?"

They looked at each other.

Ruby sighed. "I don't know. But if it's supposed to happen then someone wanting to dive in will show up."

"Yes, you're right, if it's supposed to happen, it will. That's all you and I can hope for."

"True. Okay, let's get back. I have a feeling I'm needed." They headed for the car. "It's exciting, though. Really is. And I'm enjoying watching the changes."

Josie Jane grinned. "Me, too, as is everyone who was out there helping get ready today. And like we were talking before, there is a lot of potential that could come from this first customer dance. It'll be fun to watch, and we'll be glad we didn't commit to too much other than trying to draw customers to town."

And she knew she was right. This would have been

too much for either of them, and it would take someone who could concentrate on a B&B and love it who could open one, especially if it was as big as this house.

"All I can say," Ruby said, "is if it's meant to happen, it will. Just look at that Genna coming to town, and then this is happening. And I don't really know the young woman who owns this house, but if she were to come to town and see the potential, she might be the one to make it happen."

"Maybe so. But I can already tell you it's going to be fun watching the dance next weekend and seeing what comes of it." They reached her car, and she couldn't help smiling. "And you and I might not get into the bed and breakfast gig but we can root for things to happen and our town to grow. And I'm really rooting for West and Genna."

"Me too," Ruby said.

They both chuckled as they got into the car. It was fun thinking about romance and how it could bloom in their little town and just maybe if they had events like this one coming up more often, they could watch it happen.

CHAPTER ELEVEN

West stood outside the barn later that evening, after the day in town helping put up lights. He could see his red, white, and blue Texas flag-painted mailbox at the end of the drive, and he wanted to see Genna's car coming up to it and turning in to the driveway.

And just as he thought that, she came around the curve, and his heart went crazy. He had a mama goat moving around one minute and laying down the next as it waited and wanted to give birth. He'd been hoping she held off so Genna could watch the babies' first moments after arriving. She would enjoy it and who knew, maybe watching the baby goats being born would cause her to think about how she would like to have some one day. Maybe that would help her to stop pushing him away.

Maybe she had something bad happen in her life. But possibly seeing these cute babies being born, she'd think about her life, married with children. He had begun thinking about that all the time. And his eyes were set on Genna.

He was in too deep and he knew it, but there was no going back.

He watched her drive down the lane, then pull up next to his truck, which was on the outside of the cattle guard where he'd told her to park. The entrance to this part of the barn was separate from all the other goats, giving them time alone and giving the mother goat the space she needed without a lot of romping and playing going on. He walked over to open her door but she already had it opened and was standing up when he arrived. She wore well-worn jeans that looked about as comfortable as her own skin. She wore a pale-blue shirt tied at the waist, and her dark hair hung in slack curls around her shoulders.

And he was spellbound watching her.

She smiled, and he smiled back and wanted to take her into his arms and kiss the fire out of her. *Would he?*

Would she feel anything for him if he did kiss her? Or would he lose her? He wasn't taking any chances, so he tucked his fingers in his pockets. "Glad you made it. She's about to have them, so we need to get in there. I'm pretty sure two babies are coming. There's always a chance for three and sometimes four."

"Seriously?"

He laughed. "Yup. But two is my guess."

"I can't believe it. You had a feeling tonight was the night."

"Yup, so come on. You're going to enjoy this."

He slipped his hand under her elbow and gently led her to the barn, enjoying the feel of her soft skin and the electric fire a simple touch of her skin sent through him. He'd told himself to keep his hands to himself but before he could stop himself, he'd made the move. Thankfully she hadn't told him to step away and drop his hand. It was a small step but maybe…just maybe…she was coming around to him.

The goats had gathered at the fence and were watching them and talking to them in their goat language as they past and she chuckled. "They are all so wonderful. But I can see why you told me we'd be entering a different way."

"Yep, don't need that much distraction when the babies are being born." Or when he wanted as much of her attention as he could get.

They entered the big red barn, and he led her to the well-lit stalls that had a sliding door that separated this section from the rest of the barn when needed like now. There lay the mama goat. She looked up at them with big eyes and let out a small, "Maa."

"Aw, so sweet. She knows what's about to happen and is ready, and excited I think."

"I think you're right. You arrived just in time, like I hoped you would. Goats don't often need help but after they're born, we'll clean them up and swaddle them like a baby and rock them back and forth to make sure their lungs are clear."

"Wow." She smiled, and it dug deep. "I'm so glad I came out here. Thanks for asking me."

She didn't look standoffish or emotional like she had earlier, and he hoped that wasn't a bad sign. He had enjoyed knowing she felt something he might be feeling, even if it was hard on her. At least if she felt something for him, maybe he had a chance.

"Here goes," he said as the goat grunted and moved, then pushed.

"Oh look, it's a bubble."

He chuckled. "Yep, a baby goat is born in a bubble. And then you'll see, when it's out completely, the bubble will lose its air, and the baby will either be freed from it by the mama or by me. Just to make sure it can breathe." And as he spoke, the mother let out another cry that was her forcing the baby out and it slid to the ground. He stepped in and cleared the air path, watching the cute little fella moving awkwardly as it got used to being in an open space and not cramped up inside his mom with its brother or sister...or both.

As he cleared the slimy leftover balloon film from what he now saw was a girl, the mama turned so she could get a look at her and give it a few licks. Then West picked the baby up, wrapping it in the small towel he had hung on the stall, and cleaned the soft, wet baby off. He grabbed another towel and swaddled it and gently rocked back and forth, and watched the look of delight on Genna's face as she looked up from the little kid to him.

"You're good with her," she said, her voice soft.

"I've been helping baby goats for a long time. You should have seen my gram. Boy, did she adore when babies were born. And she loved that I enjoyed it as much as she did. My brothers enjoy seeing the goats but none of them enjoy them like they do horses and cows. Me, I guess I have a lot of Gram in me."

Her eyes twinkled as she smiled at him, and his heart throbbed as his hands stroked the baby and rocked it to help make sure her lungs were cleared. But his thoughts were on the way Genna looked at him. *Oh, how he loved her.*

"Thank you for asking me to come help. I...I love this. And you have a special way with them. Your gram would be proud."

He smiled. "I hope so. You can come hold her if you want. We're about to have another little kid, and I can be ready for it if you help with this little sweetheart."

"Oh, yes." She stepped into the open stall gate and opened her arms as if not caring if she got dirty or wet, just wanting to hold the sweet little kid.

He gently shifted the baby into her open arms, and she cupped it just like he had been, clearly having paid attention to what he had been doing.

He smiled at her. "You're good at this."

"No, you are. Oh, I see another bubble," she said as her eyes had shifted from him to behind him.

He turned and sure enough, the second baby bubble was emerging. And within short moments, they had the second baby, and he and Genna and the mama goat were all smiling contently as they took care of the newborns. Genna had hers ready as the mom came nudging and he was getting the second one ready to rock. "Go ahead and lay it there in the hay and let them get familiar. And then I'll give you this cute little fella. I'll clean up while you get him breathing good before we set him down to join his family."

She took the little fella and cuddled him close. And he wanted to take her into his arms and cuddle her close. But instead he smiled at her, then turned toward the wet hay, grabbed a thick thronged rake, and got to work.

Later, they stood outside the now closed gate and

watched the little kids as they nursed from their mom.

"I loved it," Genna said, her words barely audible in the stillness of the room.

"I'm glad. So do you want to go in and get something to drink or eat?"

She laid her head on her arms that were crossed on the fence. Her beautiful eyes studied him. "You are a special man, West. I loved this so much, but—"

Unable to stop himself or just wanting to feel her lips against his more than anything, he leaned forward and covered her beautiful mouth with his.

* * *

Genna couldn't move as West leaned forward and kissed her. Her heart pounded and her pulse went haywire. But she was walking on clouds as she gave in to the longing she'd had since their moments on Main Street.

She loved this man, his life, and especially his little goats. *But what, oh what was she going to do about that?*

CHAPTER TWELVE

The crowd that showed up for the dance was amazing. Genna hadn't even gone home after work. Instead, she'd grabbed one of Red's wonderful BLTs to eat. The man could make bacon, lettuce, and tomatoes taste more fabulous than anything she could cook. She could have gone home but instead she touched up her makeup in the dressing room mirror and changed clothes, then stayed in town in case anyone getting ready needed her. Poor Ruby and Red had to be worn out already because the town had been busy, and so had they. Her store had also been busy, but she'd been thankful for it because she had needed busy to take her mind off the emotions that had plagued her since the evening with West, watching those sweet kid goats be born. *And then the kiss.* Oh, how she had loved every moment of being with that man. When he'd kissed her, everything had stopped; there was nothing in that moment except the feel of his lips against hers, kissing her as if she meant everything in the world to him. It had been perfect.

And she had run.

Thankfully, he hadn't chased her around town, pressuring her to face reality. He had told her when she'd quickly made excuses and left him after that heart-stealing kiss that he would give her space. Her fear must have been clear in her actions. And he had done exactly as he'd said, because she hadn't seen him since.

Now, as she sat in the booth, looking out over the decorated town, she wished he would pull up and park his truck right there in the parking space outside the diner's window. That he would walk straight into the diner and ask her what was wrong.

She was running and she knew it—but would she tell him that? Admit how much loving him scared her?

"You sure do look deep in thought," Ruby said as she stopped by and refilled her tea glass without even asking. "You've been a bit tense the last few days.

What's going on?"

She looked up, startled. "Have I been?"

Ruby chuckled, and considering at the moment the place was less busy because it was in-between normal mealtimes, she sat down in the cushioned seat across the table. "Yes, you have been. What is going on? I'll be frank. I've also noticed that West hasn't been around this week. The man loves breakfast and lunch here and is usually here for at least one of those meals—my husband can cook better than anyone. But you're actually sitting where West loves to sit. And it's because all the booths on this window have a view of the road. But that particular seat has the clearest view of your store window and door. And that is where he likes to sit. Before you moved to town, he sat anywhere in the diner I seated him. But you showed up and he began requesting this table." She smiled. "I'm a quick learner and if at all possible, I started saving it for when he would show up."

She was stunned and thrilled by Ruby's words, knowing he had obviously been sitting here because of the view of her store. Watching to see her if she came outside. "He hasn't been in lately?"

"Nope, not since the day we decorated. His brother said he's been busy, that he has some new baby goats and told him he needed to give them some care."

"Yes, they're cute and sweet." *But did they need extra care or was he just wanting to stay away after she'd left after that wonderful kiss?*

"So, you've seen them?"

"The babies? Yes, I went out and watched them be born, and then he showed me how to take care of them right after they came out." Her eyes teared up; she looked down quickly and blinked hard before lifting her head back up.

Ruby clearly had seen the tears. "Is everything all right?"

"Ye—no," she finished, unable to lie.

"It's obvious you two have something special going on, so what's wrong?"

"Me. I'm what's wrong. I love this town. What if I give in to the feelings I have and then he walks away? Will that mess up me being here, calling this wonderful town home?"

"I knew it! You love him. And no, you two look like you were meant for each other, and you shouldn't run away from that. In all the years we've owned this place, I've never seen a man sit consistently in my diner, watching for the sight of a woman. But West has watched you since you moved here, and I was beginning to think he was never going to act on how he felt. Honey, if he's let you in on how much he cares, then you have nothing to fear. The man is in love. At least, that's what I've come up with about his actions. And the other day, watching him help you with those lights, I knew my instincts were right."

Genna's head began to swim with all the things holding her back. "But what if we're wrong? What if he decides I'm not the right one?"

Ruby placed her palm on Genna's shoulder and squeezed gently as their eyes met. "He won't do that, not as far as I can tell. But the truth is, until you let him in, you'll never know what the ending will be."

Genna nodded, her heart tightened because she knew this was true, but what was she going to do about it? Could she take that chance?

She was still thinking about that later as the dance crowd gathered on the street and she was greeted by a hugely smiling Audrey. "Genna, this is wonderful. I was so excited to come here, and this is my daughter Jasmine."

A beautiful woman who looked to be somewhere in her thirties, around Genna's age, but she did not look very enthusiastic. Still, her medium brown hair was thick and hung in waves over her shoulders and down midway of her back. She wore a pair of jeans with a lacy shirt that had come from Genna's online store. So she was a customer too. Genna smiled and noticed many of the cowboys glancing their way, looking at Jasmine. She was going to have plenty of dance offers. "It's nice to meet you," she said, holding her hand out to the newcomer.

Jasmine shook her hand and gave a faint smile. "My mother insisted I come to the dance, and we did a little bit of shopping before it started."

"Did you find anything you liked?"

"She's not into antiques and such," Audrey said. "But as you can see she loves your shop's clothes, but we got here a bit late to get in. Some of the stores stayed open a little late to accommodate us."

She heard the disappointment in Audrey's words. "I'm sorry, I closed a little early because I had a lot to do helping with set up. But Jasmine, I recognized that shirt the moment I saw you. You make it look great."

Jasmine smiled more enthusiastically though not exuberantly. "I do love your clothes. Mom got me to start shopping online and I wasn't instantly a buyer. You have great taste."

Flattered, she smiled. "Well thanks, that means you do too."

They all laughed at that and Jasmine's mood seemed to ease up.

"Like I mentioned the last time we talked, she's looking for a job. She did move to Marble Falls and right now she's with her aunt and uncle," Audrey said. "If you ever think you might need someone to help in your wonderful store please keep her on your list."

"Mom, don't…"

Audrey shot her a glance. "I'm just trying to help you get a fresh start."

"I can do that on my own." The lighter mood had dissipated instantly and she gave Genna a look of apology. "Sorry. I'm not sure what my plans are at the moment. But Mom is driving me a little overboard with her worry. She forgets that I'm an adult sometimes." She gave a light smile and there was a softness in her eyes.

Genna liked it. The lady was annoyed by her mom's pushing but it was obvious she was trying not to get upset about it like she'd done momentarily earlier."

"I hope it all goes well for you. Believe me, I totally understand relocating. I did it when I came here. I needed it terribly and this place just drew me in the moment I drove into town."

"Really? I'm here a little against my will, hadn't planned on relocating—" she shot a glance at her mom, who patted her on the back.

"You're doing what you need to do. Now, let's go mingle. I'm ready for some tea or something. Thanks again for all of this, Genna," Audrey said.

Jasmine gave her a small smile. "If you led this event, you did great. I promise I'll try to have a good time." She winked as she walked away with her mom and left Genna smiling.

There was something going on in her life but she was trying to deal with it and deal with her mother's over-the-top attempt to help. Genna couldn't help but wonder what had happened, then thought back to her conversation that day in the store with Audrey. She'd wondered the same thing that day. Had she too had a breakup and needed to change her address? Or maybe she just wanted to move and as her mother had originally said, needed a change and looking for romance?

She sighed and glanced around the growing crowd and didn't see West. Instead of relief filling her, a torn feeling of longing splayed through her.

* * *

By the time the Saturday night dance had arrived, West was ready. He'd given Genna some time, and now it was time for her to stop finding excuses not to be around him. She'd kissed him that night of the baby goats being born, and then, she'd thanked him for such a wonderful night and she'd left. Left him standing in the doorway of the barn, watching her taillights disappear down the lane and wondering whether they'd really kissed and whether what he'd thought he'd felt had really existed. And if it did, was she going to act on it or run? Act on it or hide from the fact that she loved him? Because there was no way she could have kissed him the way she had without love being involved.

But, tonight was the night he planned to get her to face what was between them.

He and all his brothers drove their own trucks to town. He parked beside Dustin and they walked up the street together.

"You look like you're going on a mission." Dustin stared at him as they walked toward the area where people were spread about, getting things ready and some waiting for the party to begin.

"I guess I am." He was, and he was determined that tonight he wasn't sitting back and being the friend. He'd said he would, but he knew he had to know whether there could ever be anything between him and Genna. If she said no, then he'd have to just step back and find a way to give her the space she wanted…and that might be stepping way back.

"Okay, so hold up, brother." Dustin grabbed his arm and pulled him to a halt. "You look wild. Like your mind is running on a rampage and you might not be thinking straight."

He stared at his brother, then decided maybe he might need a moment to pull himself off the cliff. "Look, I love Genna. And I'm going to tell her."

"Well, that's a big step. I'm not ready for anything like that yet but good for you. But, shouldn't you look happy about it?"

"She might not feel the same way. But I need to know one way or the other."

"I get it. So, you were really helping her decorate the other day, then you had the night with the goats, and you both were just talking and laughing. So I'm figuring that she probably feels the same way. If that's the case, why do you look like you're on the march to a funeral?"

"I'm not. I'm nervous." He slapped a hand to his neck and rubbed. "She thinks we're just friends."

"Oh." His brother grimaced. "So, you're rushing this? That might not be good."

"No…maybe. Look, I just need to know." Was he rushing? Was he risking everything with impatience?

"I understand. I'd probably feel the same way if I ever had this kind of feeling about a woman. But you need to relax and let out some of that pressure you have stiffening you up inside or this could go south on you. You could scare her off."

"Might already have done that." He sucked in a deep breath and forced his shoulders to unstiffen.

Dustin gave him a squeeze on the shoulder. "There you go, loosening up. Now, give me a grin. I mean it, smile."

He forced the corners of his lips up and his brother chuckled, which to West's surprise made him smile.

"There's my big brother. I can remember when you would flop your hand on my shoulder and tell me to smile and you wouldn't stop until I did."

West laughed remembering those days. "Yeah, you always got stuck on sadness when we were boys."

"I did tend to get attached to things, lizards, those

goats you love, people…seeing them hurt or dying was always hard. But West, you were always the one who stepped up and knew how to help me get over burying a pet, burying our grandparents. You understood me and helped better than anyone. Maybe it was because you were barely a year older than me and were closer to knowing my feelings. Whatever it was, you helped me and I want to help you if possible. "

Dustin did have deep feelings, and West had always wondered if something had gone on in Dustin's life that he or any of his brothers didn't know about. Or was it just that he felt things deeply? He couldn't push that train of thought at the moment but maybe after he got things with Genna figured out he'd press his brother on that. Now, he couldn't do anything but find Genna.

"I'm going to get out of your way so you can find the woman on your heart. You're a great man, West. And I'm rooting for you."

He smiled at his barely a year younger than him brother. "Thanks. I needed that. I guess I was a bit too uptight."

Dustin chuckled. "Nothin' new. You were that way

all our life. That's why you and those little goats get along so well. You can watch them romp and play and relax. But if I was digging into all the bookwork and bills and all that part of our business, I might be in your situation. So, yeah, that pretty Genna might be better to relax you than watching those goats play." His smile leveled out to a more serious look that dug deep. "Maybe one day you'll have the real thing playing in that yard and maybe that's what you have on your mind. And we've all noticed when we're with you that you always seem calmer when you're sitting in the booth at Mulberry's with your attention on the shop next door."

West grinned, tension easing from him. "That obvious, huh?"

"Yep. Now, I'm going to get a drink and start roaming around since the music is starting up. I'm going to find a few gals to dance with tonight. I saw a really pretty gal here a few minutes ago that I don't recognize so I'm thinking the town's plan is working. Could be interesting." Dustin shot him a grin then headed away.

"Have fun," West said as he watched his brother head out, and then he scanned the area and saw Genna handing a plate of cookies to Beatrice Ratcliff, the older owner of the knitting store. She was a small lady sitting in a chair beside Arabella Samuels, the owner of the bakery—who Genna also handed a plate of refreshments to. She was great at helping others, even his little kids. He stepped forward and headed her way.

"Hi ladies," he said as he reached them. They smiled widely up at him and Genna turned, completely surprised by his voice. He smiled at her then looked at the older ladies. "Y'all look like you're going to have fun tonight. Are you going to dance?"

Beatricesmiled. "You see my bag? After we eat these cookies sweet Genna brought us, we're going to knit. Would you like to pull a chair up and help?"

Genna laughed, drawing his own smile when he met her sparkling eyes.

"What, you don't think I can?"

"Come on, sit down," Arabella said, watching him and then Genna. "Nope, never mind. You need to take this sweet lady out there to the dance floor. We'll knit and watch the two of you burn that dance floor up for us. Right, Beatrice?"

"Right. Great idea. Genna has been busy all evening helping everyone get set up, and then she's been setting our chairs up and bringing us cookies. She needs to have some fun, and you look more than able to do that."

He hadn't expected that. "Will you dance with me, Genna?" He held his hand out and peered into her beautiful wavering eyes. *Please dance with me.*

"Go on, have fun." Arabella smiled encouragingly. "You've done enough work. Now go."

She looked from the ladies back to him, and then she slipped her hand into his. "Okay. You ladies are persuasive."

Beatricelaughed. "You sure it's not that smile on that handsome face? Go. This Tim McGraw song that just started is a favorite of mine."

"Mine too," Arabella agreed. "Now go on. Enjoy, you two."

He smiled and led Genna out to the area where couples were dancing. He slipped his arm around her waist as he held her other hand in his, and then he led them into two-stepping slowly with the tune. She slipped into the rhythm easily, not looking at him for the first few steps. And then her gaze met his.

"You've been busy. I'm glad you got some encouragement to dance with me. Thanks." His words were low, their heads just a few inches apart, and the temptation to kiss her again was strong.

"I don't know if this is a good idea."

His arm around her waist tightened. He never wanted to let her go. "It was a great idea. Come on, Genna, I haven't been able to get you off my mind. Tell me you don't want to come back out to the ranch, that you just came because we are friends and nothing more. Because I don't believe you."

She sucked in a sharp breath. "Why are you doing this out here in the middle of everyone? Your brothers are all around, and I think someone said your parents are here somewhere."

"I haven't seen them yet, but they did make it in and are supposed to be coming tonight. Honestly, my mind has been on nothing but you. Seeing you, holding you like I am now as we dance a slow song. That's all I've thought about."

"West, don't—"

"Look, let's just have fun. I understand you might not feel the same way and that I told you just being friends would be fine, but I was wrong on my part. So, just so you know, I'd like to live my life with you by my side. And if that can't happen, well, I guess I have to live with it. But I couldn't go on pretending that being friends will satisfy me."

She'd stopped dancing at his words. His crazy but true words that had probably just ruined the future that he'd started dreaming about. He thought the music was still playing, but he couldn't be sure because his good sense was yelling loud and clear that he was an idiot.

"I need to go help Millie Watts oversee the dessert table—she, um, she might not be able to make them, but she was pretty blunt about being the one to oversee it. She's not a dancer and wants nothing whatsoever to do with a fella… You know, she was happy once for a short time and it didn't last, so she's chosen, like me, to live life on her own, with her own dreams her responsibility and not dependent on anyone else. Like me. West, she's like me. She just knew love and lost it, and I thought I had love and lost that, but I found this town and I just can't give up the happiness I've found here, and she feels the same way. She hasn't told me that but I was watching her today, and I figured it out. She and I are alike. And if she can make it, so can I."

Then she turned and walked away.

And he just stood there, alone, and knew he'd messed up in a stupid, unbelievable way.

CHAPTER THIRTEEN

"You and that handsome West looked like y'all were having a good time—until you suddenly weren't. What happened?" Millie asked the moment Genna strode to her table and moved behind it to stand beside the long, tall, strong-willed woman.

The woman she needed to learn from.

Genna waved a hand, as if brushing a fly from her cheek. "Nothing. I just needed my space."

"That so? Well, then welcome over here at the serving table. It's nice to have the table and the drinks between us and the party." Her words were drawled out in a slow, knowing way.

"Good. That's perfect for me. I'm not dancing again. It's me enjoying this pretty little town and my customers *and* new friends like you. And also Josie

Jane, Ruby, and those two sweet ladies over there." She nodded toward Arabella and Beatrice, who were talking and laughing as they knitted and watched the couples dancing. They both looked over at her as if sensing her thoughts of them, and both scowled a tiny bit and shook their heads, clearly disappointed in her leaving West out on the dance floor.

"They don't look too happy," Millie said. "You did seem perturbed at West. Everyone was watching you two, and I can tell you from an earlier conversation before you arrived that there was hope that you and West might be having some feelings about each other."

Her breath caught at Millie's words just as a young boy came up to the table.

"Can I have a drink?" asked a young boy who'd raced up to the table, giving Genna an excuse not to answer immediately.

"Sure you can. What do you want?"

He stared at the cans iced down and pointed at a bright-colored Big Red soda. "That'll do it."

She chuckled, unable not to, the boy was grinning so big. "I like them too. Here you go." She handed him the cold can.

His eyes sparkled and as he took it, he hitched his brow. "That's good, 'cause I'm getting it for her—" He nodded toward a young girl standing over near someone who looked like her mother, because they looked similar. "She's new in town and cute, and I think this will help her like me."

Then he spun away and headed toward the little girl. He was only about eight, it looked like, and she was about the same age. As he approached her, she saw him and smiled. Instantly he held out the canned drink and a big smile burst across her cute little face.

"Young love is sweet," Millie said, her voice soft and wistful. "Her mother is the one who just came to town and owns the big house that Ruby told me she'd thought about trying to buy, but when she saw it, Ruby knew it was perfect for a bed-and-breakfast but too big for her to open. Why she had even thought about it is beyond my understanding. Their Mulberry Diner keeps them busy the majority of the time."

Thank goodness this was a new direction for the conversation. Genna studied the tanned woman with straight black hair with long bangs swept to the side so it hung gently along her face as she looked down at her daughter. She smiled at the look of shining eyes of her little girl and the nice boy handing her the drink. "So is she here to live or just to check everything out?"

"I don't know. One thing I don't do is ask too many questions. I figure if someone wants to offer me some info, they will. If not, I'm just fine with what they give me. Like you. I know you're not wanting to talk about what is going on between you and that handsome, good goat-loving cowboy, but if you need someone to talk to who keeps her mouth closed, I'm here. Been there myself and had no one, but I made it anyway—just thought I'd offer."

The words brought a surge of tears to the brink of Genna's eyes, but she managed to keep them back. This wonderful lady did understand and had been through heartbreak...*am I?* "Thank you."

"Life is full of floating happiness and dark holes. I've been in both and found my footing on the solid ground in-between. You'll find your way. Just take it slow and maybe even pray about it...that's what I did, and I'm happy...content and know I was blessed deeply for a little while. And I just want to add that I'm grateful for that short while. Very grateful."

They held each other's gazes and then, unable to help herself, Genna wrapped her arms around the tall woman and hugged her tight as her throat clogged with emotion. "Thank you," she whispered, her voice cracking.

Millie hugged her back, patting her on the back. "You're a strong gal, and I like that. You'll be fine. But I have to say, I don't know about that handsome goat lover. He looked about as sad as a man can be when he turned and walked through the crowd and disappeared down the dark side road."

Startled, Genna straightened and wiping dampness from beneath her eyes, she stared toward the crowd, her gaze searching for West.

"He's gone. So have a drink and maybe some desserts and let this lovely music soothe you."

Genna couldn't hear what was playing as she reached for a soda, just needing something to do with her hands. Hands that wanted to ram through her hair while she screamed at herself about what she'd done.

* * *

By the time the party was over and she'd helped clean up and headed home, Genna was worn out and so sad as she parked her car and got out. The moon was bright and she stared up at it…remembering sitting out here that night with West.

How was he?

Sighing, she spun and headed inside, needing to get ready for bed and hoping she slept—which she was pretty sure wouldn't happen.

And she was right, because by the time the sun came up, she'd already had three cups of coffee and was sitting outside in the front yard, staring across the pasture at the place where the fallen tree had been and the new fence now stood. And the cattle were grazing all about. Oh, how she'd enjoyed that day of helping West.

She'd gone over it and over it and fought the feelings that clung to her like a stinging swarm of bees—wasps, it was hurting so bad. His words, so open and direct, hadn't left her. And she hadn't been able to let them go. *They fit.*

He was looking for someone who could love his goats and his life as much as he did but also someone he could love as much…no, more than…he loved those cute little creatures that made him and her both grin like kids. *Kids.* The word echoed through her. Those sweet, playful little goats were known as kids, and she loved them and wanted to be a part of their lives. But she also wanted real kids, children of her own one day. Suddenly, she sprang from the chair, dropping her coffee cup as she gasped.

"I want it with West. I want a life with *him.*"

She spun and raced toward the house. She had to get over there. She had to set this right. This was what she wanted and why, oh why, was she letting that long-forgotten two-timer run her life?

Ruin her life when she now understood she'd been blessed to get kicked to the curb by him, the man she'd thought she'd loved. She wasn't going to let him dictate how she spent the rest of her life any longer. Not when she totally and completely knew now she hadn't loved him—hadn't known what real love felt like. He had blessed her with his actions, she smiled, laughed at the very idea that not marrying him had been a blessing and she just now realized it.

She'd woken up. Loving West had done that, and thank goodness for that.

Smiling, she knew now was time to take her life back. It was time to show her love to the man of her dreams and the life he had that she so wanted to embrace.

Life was too short, it was time to make dreams come true.

* * *

West stood in the midst of his goats, beside the donkey that had one on his back that was dancing as if today were a great day to play and celebrate. Not for him. But watching the antics of this little crew and the patience of the donkeys helped him know even though life was going to be hard after Genna made it clear they were done, at least he had this happy, fun group to find some smiles in as he took care of them.

He heard an engine and knew a car or truck must be coming up his drive, so he took a deep breath and tried to force his expression to one that didn't tell whoever it was how much pain and sadness he was struggling with at the moment. And then the car came over the cattle guard, and he saw her inside as she slammed on the brakes and threw open the door.

His heart flew up and slammed to the top of his head, making him dizzy. The kids raced toward her, squealing and jumping and kicking as they surrounded her as she came his way. He couldn't move, just watched as the happy babies slammed into her legs. Instantly, she went down, squealing with either happiness or tears—it was hard to decipher—as he jolted forward to help get her out from under the landslide of happy little wiggle worms telling her they'd missed her just as much as he had.

He pushed them aside, now hearing the sounds she made were laughs of delight. As she looked up at him with glowing eyes, hope filled him as he took her hands and gently tugged her to stand.

"I love you," she gasped. "I do. And I'm so sorry I tried to run you off, West. Please tell me you still love me."

He grinned, then nodded as he pulled her into his arms and let his lips settle where they belonged—on her soft, sweet lips that bonded with his just as they were meant to be.

And as they both joined into the kiss with joyful glee, the sounds of little and big goats sang, as if this were the beginning of all their dreams coming true.

And it was.

EPILOGUE

"It smells wonderful in here," Genna said as she washed her hands at the kitchen sink of West's house...which would become her home soon.

West came up behind her and slipped his arms around her as she dried her hands on one of his dishtowels. "I have to say it does. With Grams roast and your amazing cherry pie this place is going to blow my brothers and my parents away when they get here." He leaned his head in and kissed the side of her neck sending a warm rush of delight flying through her.

She turned toward him, so very happy to be here with him and excited about what they were about to tell his family, who were coming for Sunday lunch. "Are you sure none of them know?"

He grinned and popped a teasing kiss to her lips.

"They do not know. I've kept my mouth shut all week— wanting only to see you and hold you when we were both off work and enjoying spending time together. I can tell you they are all going to be happy. Mom will probably hug you so tight I'll have to rescue you. She'll be so thrilled."

She smiled then kissed him with a teasing peck. "My mom and stepdad are thrilled, and I know Daddy is too, looking down on us from his place high in the sky."

His gaze dug deep. "Then we're making everyone happy. Including me."

"And me."

"Especially all those little goats romping around out there that you have played with all week when you came out to dinner. You're a hit with them, you know."

"I love them. This was all meant to be, West." She believed that with all of her heart.

The sound of trucks arriving drew them from leaning together against the kitchen counter and walking arm in arm to the door. There came a herd of trucks as all of his family were coming to lunch. And they would learn the exciting news that they were having a wedding in a month—only waiting that long so her mom and stepdad could get home from their latest trip. They had offered to end the trip and come directly here, but Genna had told them not to. She and West were keeping everything quiet until after lunch with his family, and then they would let them know the happy news.

Genna had no doubt that there was going to be a load of helpers from her new hometown as soon as the news got out. And from all the wonderful friends she'd made in the town business owners, especially sweet Josie Jane and Ruby. The planning of this wedding was going to be fun and filled with more excitement. She was officially the first match made in Lone Star since the dance. Even though her and West's love had started the day the idea was first expressed by her sweet customer and she shared it with Josie Jane and Ruby. Could there be more love stories that came from that idea of having a dance and inviting everyone's customers? Maybe, only time would tell.

And, she had a new store employee moving to town soon. Jasmine, the one and only daughter of Audrey, who had inspired this fun idea for the town. Genna hadn't been able to get the lady off her mind, and she knew the moment she'd said yes to marrying West that she needed help in the store because she wanted some time off to spend here on this wonderful ranch with him and all these adorable kids they would be surrounded with. And hopefully in the near future some true children of their own who would enjoy playing outside with all the rambunctious kids she could hear announcing the arrival of West's family.

He hugged her close, grinning as she looked up at him and saw his eyes dancing with excitement as he held her and watched the kids jumping and calling out to all his brothers and his mom and dad as they climbed from their vehicles. Then they were each greeted by the goats as if they were their family. She laughed with delight when his mother waved at them, then instantly bent to her knees, opened her arms, and welcomed as many of the babies that could and wanted to give her a cuddle.

"She loves them too," Genna said, delighted.

West kissed the top of her head. "Yes, you and my

mom will get along great. And I don't know if you see the gleam in all my brothers' eyes but I think our surprise isn't going to be a surprise after all." He laughed and so did she.

"It's perfect. I love it all. And I really, really love you, West. Thank you for pursuing me and waking me up to what I really wanted in my life. You and all we can create with our love together." She was looking up at him and he drew his gaze from his family, smiled widely and then dropped his lips to hers, no hurry, just a deep, loving kiss that went on and on…and if any of his family had wondered what they were here for, Genna was entirely convinced that they now knew.

Love was here to stay and it was truly her dream come true to have this sweet oh so loving cowboy to call her own.

More Books by Hope Moore

Billionaire Cowboys of Lone Star, Texas
Forever Love'n Cowboy
Sweet Love'n Cowboy
Heart Love'n Cowboy

McCoy Billionaire Brothers
Her Billionaire Cowboy's Fake Marriage
Her Billionaire Cowboy's Fake Wedding Fiasco
Her Billionaire Cowboy's Trouble in Paradise
Her Billionaire Cowboy's Secret Baby Surprise
Her Billionaire Cowboy's Second Chance Romance
Her Billionaire Cowboy Fake Fiancé
Her Billionaire Cowboy's Inconvenient Marriage Blessing

Billionaire Cowboys of True Love, Texas
Billionaire Cowboy's Runaway Bride
Billionaire Cowboy's Wedding Crasher
Her Billionaire Cowboy's Hill Country Proposal
Billionaire Cowboy Auctioned at Christmas
Billionaire Cowboy's Dream Come True

About the Author

Hope Moore is the pen name of an award-winning author who lives deep in the heart of Texas surrounded by Christian cowboys who give her inspiration for all of her inspirational sweet romances. She loves writing clean & wholesome, swoon worthy romances for all of her fans to enjoy and share with everyone. Her heartwarming, feel good romances are full of humor and heart, and gorgeous cowboys and heroes to love. And the spunky women they fall in love with and live happily-ever-after.

When she isn't writing, she's trying very hard not to cook, since she could live on peanut butter sandwiches, shredded wheat, coffee...and cheesecake why should she cook? She loves writing though and creating new stories is her passion. Though she does love shoes, she's admitted she has an addiction and tries really hard to stay out of shoe stores. She, however, is not addicted to social media and chooses to write instead of surf FB - but she LOVES her readers so she's working on a free novella just for you and if you sign up for her newsletter she will send it to you as soon as its ready! You'll also receive snippets of her adventures, along with special deals, sneak peaks of soon-to-be released books and of course any sales she might be having.

She promises she will not spam you, she hates to be spammed also, so she wouldn't dare do that to people she's crazy about (that means YOU). You can unsubscribe at any time.

Sign up for my newsletter at:

www.subscribepage.com/hopemooresignup

I can't wait to hear from you.

Hope Moore~

Always hoping for more love, laughter and reading for you every day of your life!